POCKET
PROTECTORS

SMALL BEGINNINGS

JAMES RAD

TABLE OF CONTENTS

for Hadley, my hero

1
POCKET PROTECTORS

Reva Loreley Elbourne loved superheroes. By far, her favorite assembly of good guys and girls were known as *The Planet's Proud Protectors*. When Reva was little, she could always be found playing with the Pocket Protectors Palace Playset—a preschool version of Protectors headquarters. Everything about it was fun: the roof slide, the tire swing, the rolling wheel, the merry-go-round, the stacking barrels, and the revolving door around back.

Included in the set were 3in Protectors with pocket-shaped eyes and mouths made of plastic dot stitches. There were clips so they could go on your pocket and get shown off to friends. The action figures were fittingly called: Pocket Protectors.

Pocket Protectors were all the rage when Reva's dad was growing up in the early 1980s. A toy company called Toy Boat Toy Boat Toy Boat Toys had exclusive rights to the Clash Comics universe. They made a Pocket Protector of every hero and villain in the Clash Comics universe, from well-known to obscure. Kids collected and traded Pocket Protectors, and wore at least five on each pocket of their jeans.

Around the time Reva's dad reached middle school, the fad had died. Now Pocket Protectors are very hard to find. You can get them on eBay, but each figure costs a pretty penny.

Originally, the Pocket Protectors Palace Playset belonged to Reva's dad, James. He had kept the set for the chance that someday there would be someone like Reva who would treasure it as he did. The suggested age on the box was four and up. So on the day Reva turned four, the toy was hers. Awesome gift aside, Reva's fourth birthday wasn't a happy one. Not like her previous three. For on Reva's fourth birthday, her dad disappeared.

James Elbourne was a robotics engineer. Reva didn't understand what the words *robotics* or *engineer* meant when she was a toddler, she only understood that he made robots—and that made him a rad dad.

No one knew for sure what happened to James. Reva will never forget the last time she saw him—he was still in his pajamas! He had just cleared the spider webs from the playset's original packaging. Box flaps were loose, corners caved. But the condition of the set itself was excellent, after twenty-five years in storage, between Reva's Grandma's attic and theirs. James was thrilled.

Decals stayed stuck. Contraptions went on working. The only visible blemish was a minor nick on the Protector-jet. Even the Pocket Protectors had endured. Listed on eBay, the complete set could have sold for hundreds. But Reva valued it way more.

Reva inherited James's entire collection of Pocket Protectors that totaled in the hundreds. Four of which came with the Palace. Si Q was a supergenius who could create and manipulate computer systems. Ursa Double-Major was an astronomer-turned-superheroine who could summon or take the real-life form of any animal, mythological god, or creature that a star constellation represents. Julioception, in his first iteration, was a 1950s Latin American pop star who had gained complete control over the five senses and sometimes even the sixth; he could heighten or lower his senses or the senses of those nearby. Talent Master was a virtually invisible being who could borrow a talent from any non-superpowered person within a mile radius and multiply its effect by one hundred.

The action figure that showed the most wear was Re-Lo Kate, James's favorite Protector. A smeared left eye was proof that he played with her the most. Re-Lo is the only core Protector that was sold separately from the playset. James had a fond memory of the day he received his Re-Lo as a surprise gift from his uncle.

James loved Re-Lo so much he even snuck a nod to her in his daughter's name—*Re*va *Lo*reley. Amy, his wife and Reva's mom, didn't catch what he did there until after Reva was born; Amy purely liked the name for how it sounded.

Re-Lo Kate's backstory was told in *Re-Lo Kate #1* (1941). Kate Locey was a secret agent who ended a series of impossible thefts carried out by mad scientists. How they kept getting away scot-free was the mystery. Turned out they were using a machine that could shift a person from one location to another (for example: a thief from a secret hideout to a bank vault). When the jig was surely up, the chief scientist triggered a self-destruct mechanism. The resulting explosion transferred the machine's function to Locey. It was during her recovery when Locey discovered that she had gained the power of teleportation; she simply thought about breakfast one morning and was instantly at the cereal cabinet. "Time to relocate!" became her—

now legendary—catchphrase.

In later comic runs, Re-Lo could bring another person somewhere with her—exactly like the machine she personified. Stillness after making a location-shift granted her invisibility. When fighting, she could harness the shift power to produce a super-strength attack.

With practice Re-Lo learned to shift back in time. She could investigate moments as a spectral sleuth (or ghost detective for the uninitiated), but was unable to interact with the world. No matter how long Re-Lo stayed in the past, she always came back to the precise moment in the present from which she blinked, as if time itself waited for her return.

Additionally, she could open portals through which the other Protectors could conference with her. This ability was years ahead of video chat, but did have a limitation: it didn't work in the past. Even in today's comics her power is more reliable than most Wi-Fi.

Re-Lo joined up with the Protectors in *The Planet's Proud Protectors #64: Constellation Wars* (1960). Ursa Double-Major's arch nemesis, Ursa Triple-Major— driven by his inferiority complex—cloned the heroine's powers and brought every animal constellation down from the sky to attack New York City. This first issue in a four-part miniseries jump-started the career of all-star comics creator Tal Boatwright III (nicknamed TB3 by fans). TB3 was the only son of the legend who founded Clash Comics, Tal Boatwright Jr.

James recapped Re-Lo's backstory while Reva moved the Re-Lo Pocket Protector with the smeared left eye joyfully around the kitchen table. A black ninja catsuit was Re-Lo's trademark look; lighter bands spiraled down and around the sleeves to arrowheads on the back of her hands. True to the comics, the bands turned different colors, like a mood ring, indicating whether Re-Lo was happy, mad, scared, or sad. Reva loved Re-Lo's choppy scarlet hair—and the element of disappearing and reappearing was going to be really fun in play stories.

Crayons were out, a Re-Lo picture underway, when suddenly Reva's dad was just … gone. His keys were still hanging from the key hook. His phone was still on the counter. And if he left on foot, he did it barefooted because all of the sneakers and shoes he owned were still in his closet. No goodbye, no note, no nothing. There was only an empty chair at the kitchen table where he had been sitting a few seconds before.

When her mom returned with her baby brother, Xavier, in one arm and a bag of groceries in the other, Reva did her best to explain it. But she was four. "Him just left." (It beat every explanation the detectives gave in the months that followed.)

After a half-year, the case went cold and authorities ended the search for James Elbourne, calling it "hopeless." It goes without saying, but during that most difficult time, Reva didn't have the heart to play with any of her dad's Pocket Protectors.

2
THE FIENDISH FOUR

Shortly after the vanishing of James Elbourne, the police and the United States Armed Forces had bigger things to worry about: real-life supervillains. It was as though well-known baddies had leapt from the pages of Clash Comics and onto our streets.

At first people thought *Arrr*son, the fire-pirate, was a crazy cosplayer taking his performance art a little too far. A wannabe YouTube celebrity with a flare for pyrotechnics. People stopped laughing, though, when the scorching swashbuckler burned down an empty Dodger Stadium while the team was on a road trip. In one warning flick of his "heat-hook," he had ignited a global panic. "Pirate-technics" was the buzzword.

Next, Hoodwinker appeared in New York City. Hoodwinker wore a dark hood and an ancient leather blindfold with black eye-coverings that he could somehow see through without ever flipping them up. Individuals or even whole crowds were tricked into believing whatever thoughts he made them think. Seats opened for Hoodwinker on the subway when fleeing riders were convinced that they had explosive diarrhea. Bank tellers let him withdraw money, and he didn't have an account. For three weeks he starred in *Cats* on Broadway, subjecting unsuspecting audiences to his horrendous acting. And he didn't refund a single ticket.

Chicago was the home of Bombastic, a thin man in a stretchy black suit who could inflate to any size, then explode. He demonstrated his power by completely obliterating the Pritzker Music Pavilion in Millennium Park for everyone to see on YouTube. Casting a shadow over every major building in the Windy City, officials had no choice but to meet his cash demands. The US Army and Air Force tried popping Bombastic with darts from a distance, but he would repeatedly break just enough wind to send their vehicles soaring for miles.

The supervillainess, Misbeehive, terrorized Houston, Texas. And misbehave she did with the thousands of bees that buzzed her yellow-and-black striped uniform. On her command the bees would swarm, once allowing her to rob all three hundred and seventy-five stores in The Galleria shopping mall.

Unfortunately for humankind, almost a year had passed and no real-life Protectors had emerged.

People stayed vigilant though. New apps marked areas where the villains were wreaking havoc, places to avoid at all costs. Unbelievably, no one had gotten seriously injured. But it was clear that the "Fiendish Four"—as they were called on the news—were gaining in strength and growing bored of getting rich. There was a strange electric current that had developed under their skin and got more visible over time; a streaking red light, like little lightning bolts coursing through their veins.

One day, the Fiendish Four joined forces to cast our biggest cities into peril simultaneously. *Arrr*son, skull-and-bones captain's hat and eyepatch all ablaze, hovered over Sleeping Beauty's castle in Disneyland—

threatening to throw the flames from his heat-hook at the children below. Hoodwinker had hundreds of tourists waiting to jump off the Empire State Building on his signal; and the tourists were sure as the wind blows that they could fly. Speaking of wind, Bombastic was providing blimp coverage over Soldier Field in Chicago—where he was the blimp. Blustering about moving the football stadium to Lake Michigan if a single Bear fan moved from his or her seat. And Misbeehive had the Space Center in Houston surrounded by bees with poison-laced stingers.

But just as doom fell over those cities and spread across the world, one by one, each supervillain vanished in a flash from the landmarks, from the news, and from existence. Bringing a collective sigh of relief. Some cheered. Some fainted. Some cried. Some hugged their children and wouldn't let go. Some thought it was too good to be true.

Then—in the midst of the confusion and shock and celebration—a man behind a star-spangled mask, sporting red-white-and-blue tights, took over every TV station from an undisclosed location.

HOAP was his name. Stood for: Hero of All People. Explained the giant *H* across his plated chest. He wasn't based on any Clash Comics character like the Fiendish Four. Nobody understood why, but he wore a red utility belt that carried a collection of Pocket Protectors: Re-Lo, Si Q, Ursa Double-Major, Julioception, and Talent Master. Same action figures from James's collection, but these had sheen. These were brand new. Influencers flooded social media with speculation that Toy Boat Toy Boat Toy Boat Toys had sponsored HOAP for a relaunch of their once-popular toy line.

In a few words, HOAP revealed to the world where the Fiendish Four had gone. "Beamed" to a cellblock inside his secret headquarters is how he put it. Then he boldly staked his claim as the first—and only—real-life super*hero*.

A website address spanned the screen: www.HOAP.com. It loaded a livestream of four glass cells with a bad guy or girl in each. That zapping red light appeared fully charged now, streaking from their fiendish heads to their fiendish toes. The livestream was a way for people to keep tabs on the Fiendish Four—to feel safe again. So normal, everyday lives could resume.

Neither police nor United States Armed Forces demanded that HOAP turn the villains over to their custody. That's because the cells were specially designed to nullify the Fiendish Four's powers. Sub-zero temperatures kept the fire-pirate, *Arrr*son, cool. Hoodwinker's cell was constructed with two-way glass; you could see him, but all he could see was the reflection of his goggled eyes staring back (his mind-control power only worked on those caught in his stare). A cell significantly narrower than the others prevented Bombastic from inflating. And Misbeehive's cell was augmented with smokers, inspired by the beekeeper's method for calming bees. The periodic smoke produced by the computerized system had the same effect on the villainess and her honey-loving followers.

Majestic statues of HOAP were promptly erected in the major cities he had saved. HOAP was the talk of the world. #HOAP broke the internet. He was a guest on every talk show. Hosted *Saturday Night Live*. Shook hands with President Obama at the White House. Artists remixed the Obama "Hope" poster with the hero's image and unique spelling of the word. No doubt about it, he truly was the Hero of All People.

3
RE-LO

Reva was five years old when HOAP locked up the Fiendish Four. From time to time, she would catch her mom checking in on the HOAP.com livestream. *Arm*son, Hoodwinker, Bombastic, and Misbeehive vanished into thin air. So it was impossible not to wonder if her dad's disappearance one year earlier were somehow connected. Difference is, the Fiendish Four reappeared in these custom cells. James was nowhere to be found. She hoped—like her mom did—that one day the panning view of HOAP's cellblock would include her dad.

When Reva missed her dad—which was often—she played with the Pocket Protectors Palace Playset. There was always a role in her stories for the entire cast of colorful characters. Si Q had a yellowish-green head shaped like an upturned butternut squash, eyes that glowed green, a unibrow of printed circuit board, and a blonde tuft of hair. Ursa Double-Major had a brown tone, purple hair in a sock bun, and a Big Dipper constellation design on her cheek. Julioception had an olive-colored square head, slick side-parted hair, and a sharp white suit. Talent Master had a shiny blue cloak and hood that obscured part of its transparent face. The Pocket Protectors were perfect little recreations of

Reva's favorite heroes, but one always got a few more turns down the trapdoor chute in the roof than the others: Re-Lo Kate.

Reva was convinced that the Re-Lo figure giggled whenever it went down the slide and shot out the side. That it frowned at the end of every playtime. That it winked the same way her dad would. She didn't dare speak of this, fearing that her mom would make her share it with the "talking doctor."

It was firmly on record that Reva's dad was obsessed with Re-Lo comics; Reva always needed those four letters in alphabet magnets to spell her first and middle names. Re-Lo was hidden in her name; stands to reason why she suspected that her dad was hidden in the action figure.

One day, while Si Q was whirling in the rooftop spinner, Ursa Double-Major was rocking in the tire swing, and Talent Master was rolling across the hardwood floor in the wheel, Re-Lo was being moved by Reva up the plastic stairs to the blue garage roof for another turn down the trapdoor chute.

But on this day, on this slide, Re-Lo never rolled out onto the floor. At first, Reva thought it must have gotten stuck. Poking down the trapdoor with one hand and up the exit with the other, her fingers touched. Wiggled them too, and even then didn't feel Re-Lo. She tipped the playset on its side, knocking Julioception off the merry-go-round and sending Si Q flying from the rooftop spinner. Putting her eye to the exit, she could see that it was clear. Confirmed: Re-Lo definitely was not stuck inside.

Reva put the playset right side up and opened the blue garage roof. No Re-Lo. It never exited the chute. It wasn't stuck. It didn't take a wrong turn. It was gone.

Vanished. "Her just left," Reva would have said a year ago.

Waterworks came next. Reva ran crying from her lilac-colored room down the hallway runner to the kitchen, where Mom was preparing her daily peanut butter sandwich. The ginger coloring and blue-green eyes Reva got from James. The heart-shaped chin—that turned red when she was upset—came from Amy. Xavier, Reva's brother, who was two years old, was a spitting image of Amy with that same heart-shaped chin, dark hair, and brown eyes.

Reva gave her mom a detailed—and blubbering—account about the incident. How Re-Lo went down through the trapdoor but didn't come out the exit. How she looked inside and the chute was empty.

Amy didn't believe her. A toy couldn't just vanish into thin air. Re-Lo had to be in Reva's room somewhere. Tangled in her pink fuzzy rug or under the dresser or bed. There was a theory Amy never said out loud: Reva was connecting her dad's disappearance to a simple case of a lost toy.

After days of searching, Reva and her mom never found Re-Lo. It wasn't tangled in her pink fuzzy rug. It wasn't under her dresser or bed. It wasn't mixed in her toy drawer with stuffed animals and puzzles. Or in her dress-up bin with this Halloween's Re-Lo costume. It wasn't in any of her desk drawers with the pink knobs. It wasn't in the living room or kitchen or Xa's room. It wasn't anywhere.

Despite turning the house inside out with no results, Amy refused to believe that Re-Lo had vanished. The feeling Reva had in her bones—that her dad *was* the Re-Lo Pocket Protector—had to stay bottled up. Otherwise, the talking doctor would call her crazy.

Reva at age five couldn't define the word *coincidence*, but she definitely would not define the past year's events—James's disappearance, the Fiendish Four, HOAP, Re-Lo—as merely that. All of it had to be connected. Somehow. In the comics, Re-Lo Kate could location-shift and go invisible and even bring someone to another place.

"Maybe Re-Lo took Daddy somewhere!" When Reva finally said what she had spent days thinking, it made her mom burst into tears.

So Reva did her best to never think it again.

4

THE CLASH COMICS CLUB

Seven years later. July 21, 2020.
San Diego Comic-Con.

According to *Guinness World Records*, San Diego
Comic-Con is the largest comic and pop culture festival
in the world. Reva has to pinch herself. Still stunned
that her friends' parents actually approved a cross-
country flight for a comic book event birthday party.
Today, Reva turns twelve; and this celebration has been
in the works since she was ten. Most of the girls she
knows just have spa parties and pizza.

Amy has always gone all out for Reva's birthdays.
That's because James disappeared on July 21, 2012,
Reva's fourth birthday. An extravagant celebration is
Amy's way of distracting from that terrible tragedy. But
this party—a West Coast trip to attend Protector
panels, writing workshops, and Clash Comics Cinematic
Universe (C3U) sneak-peek screenings—blows away
every bash from the past. Even last year's. When Amy
converted their street to a drive-in theater for a viewing
of *E.T.* (the original cut in which Elliot calls his
brother, "penis breath"). There was even a concession
stand with classic drive-in snacks.

It's the summer before sixth grade. Reva's friends

are the same friends she's had since third. A group vacation to Comic-Con is only possible because, over that stretch of time, the parents have become best friends too.

Amy delayed Reva's start to elementary school because of the struggles Reva was having with James's vanishing and the added trauma from the Fiendish Four situation. That made Reva nine in third grade, when she and her friends from Mrs. Wilmarth's class formed the Clash Comics Club. They convened at lunch and during recess to discuss the latest Protector issues and C3U tie-in novels (at least the ones their parents okayed).

Reva and her best friend, Stella Keene, founded the club. Where Reva was soft-spoken and shy, Stella was loud and outwardly silly. Personalities weren't dissimilar; it's just that expression didn't come as easily for Reva. Often Reva wished she were daring enough for the Ninja Warrior team or adding blue to her hair, the things that made Stella stand out.

Stella has always had a way of boosting Reva's confidence. If their rap song about Antarctica hadn't been a duet, Reva never would have performed it for the whole class. Never would she have petted that sand shark on the field trip to the Marine Biology Center if Stella hadn't been by her side.

Stella sang beautiful solos in chorus, drew hilarious doodles during free time, and stood on podiums at Ninja Warrior competitions. One way or another, she seemed destined to be a star.

Routine comic book store trips on Wednesdays weren't required to get a Clash Comics Club membership. Rules stated that you at least had to be a fan of Clash movies. Sam Izumi begged Reva and Stella to be in their reading club. But back at the start of third grade, Sam couldn't have named even a single Protector.

Sam has forever been super smart. Mrs. Wilmarth would ask *him* to teach students use of the Chromebooks when they did third-grade math and reading lessons online. He and Reva became fast friends the day a video game studio visited their class to demo a role-playing-game (RPG) builder.

That year Sam competed in the 2017 Nintendo World Championships. Stella slept over Reva's house and they streamed it live on Amy's laptop. Sam was one of twenty-four players to participate. He made it past shield surfing in *The Legend of Zelda: Breath of the Wild* and through a boss-section speedrun of *Metroid: Samus Returns*. The eventual champion outlasted him in a round of *Tetris* on the Game Boy. *Puyo Puyo Tetris* for the Switch was Sam's jam, so he fumbled a bit with the old-school control scheme. Making it through the regional tournaments all the way to the World Championships at the age of eight was a feat in itself.

Eleven months before Sam was born, his family moved to Franklin, Massachusetts from Japan. His grandparents still live there and he has hopes of visiting them some day. Super Mario or Pokémon—or anything Japanese or game-related—graced every article in his wardrobe.

When Sam wasn't talking about his level progression in the latest JRPG (he preferred the focus on story and turned-based combat of *Japanese* RPGs), he was telling funny stories about his cat, Meow-Meow. It was Sam's love of JRPGs, and Meow-Meow, that made Reva urge him to read Protector comics. For their over-the-top narratives and characters that had attitude and style.

And especially for Si Q's quirky cat—Gray—that could beat anyone in fighting games (as long as Gray's controller was an arcade stick).

Reva lent Sam a stack of Protector comics—the best issues from the current runs of the original five: Re-Lo, Si Q, Ursa Double-Major, Julioception, and Talent Master. Before morning-work had started the following day, Sam was the third member of the Clash Comics Club.

The same stack of books found Antonio Hayes's hands on their way back to Reva. Ant (that's what everyone called him) habitually kicked the air. Front, back, side, roundhouse. If his sensei taught the move, he would practice it. Over and over. At recess, Ant was the karate teacher. If his friends desired mastery of blocking forms 1 and 2, they knew where to go.

When Mrs. Wilmarth quizzed them, Ant would close his eyes and whisper the names of animals. Many kids thought he was weird for this. The strange behavior was actually his sensei's go-to meditation technique. Intended to steady the senses. Ant never heard the giggles because his soul was at peace. Meditation gave him the sharpness, awareness, and brainpower he needed to ace any exam. Scores were typically in the mid-eighties, but he figured without the animal meditation, they would be much, much lower.

Ant was big into *Star Wars* because his dad regularly geeked out over the original trilogy. Friends could always find him in a crowd by his orange-and-white Rebel Alliance backpack and R2D2 water bottle. Video games weren't as high on Ant's list as Sam's; he did, however, borrow his parents' tablet a fair amount to play *Minecraft*. Superheroes, well, superheroes were initially Nay's thing. Ant's brother, Nay, and Reva's brother, Xa, attended the same preschool. It's there where the Hayes household began their absorption of comic book knowledge.

Ant took the stack of Protector comics from Sam and dug in after school. The text that Ant's mom sent to Amy was funny: *He won't go to bed. Still has Julioconception (sp?) and Relo Katelyn (sp?) to read.*

Amy replied: *He can keep them as long as he needs.* (She didn't bother correcting the character names.)

Mrs. Wilmarth could see it in Ant's eyes when the morning bell rang—he had stayed up late. Really late. The stack of comics had been read and returned to Reva's desk. And Ant was now the fourth member of the Clash Comics Club.

5
COMIC-CON

This is the Clash Comics Club's first official meeting outside of Franklin, MA. Reva, Stella, Sam, and Ant are assembled under the palm trees across the street from the San Diego Convention Center. The bright morning sun casts four shadows that are significantly longer than they were in third grade.

In these San Diego rays, Reva's auburn hair is deeper than ever. Freckles dot the bridge of her nose and under her blue-green eyes where they weren't in younger years. Take away Amy's heart-shaped chin and Reva at age twelve is a dead ringer for her dad.

Reva planned out her daily apparel for the convention well in advance. An appropriate collection of graphic tees. Day One: Re-Lo jumping out of a comic-panel motif. Said out loud it would sound dumb, but a piece of her dad is with her when she wears a Re-Lo shirt.

Little by little, Reva has come out of her shell. But she may never be so bold to go blue with her hair like Stella's timeless, signature style. Stella may be last in order of height, but what she doesn't come up short on is silliness. Every situation, it seems, gets an instant song to go with it:

We're not even in yet and
there's lots of weird stuff
A fat guy in a mask who
doesn't look very buff

Comic-Con is so fun
Comic-Con is so fun
Comic-Con is so fun
Comic-Con is so EP-IC!

Sam is on his phone. Tooling around in the Comic-Con app. Stella's weird songs don't faze him at all anymore. "Guys, the 'Nanotechnology in Sci-Fi: Fact or Fiction' prez starts in a half-hour."

Sam's long, straight black bangs hide much of his larger-than-normal-size forehead. You'd think his Mario and Pokémon tees grew with him since his taste in clothing hasn't changed a bit.

YouTube celebrity status is what Sam's after. And he's close. People tune in for his mad gaming skills and stay for his sharp wit and fan interactions. Reva hates his constant video blogging. For this reason, Sam made a promise not to, in the form of a birthday gift.

Snap! Snap! Never said he'd refrain from taking selfies. San Diego Convention Center adorned with colorful comic book banners … um … Sam would be a lame cyberstar if he didn't post this. One hundred thousand followers are hanging on his feeds. Providing entertaining insights is an obligation to nerds far and wide. Momentous reveals are about to shake the comic world and fans deserve his thoughts on the matters.

Antonio has shot up taller, making his shortened name, Ant, cooler in an ironic sort of way. Though Ant's red belt is at home, his meditation technique travels. He's learned to steady his senses without listing off animals. Nevertheless, the massive crowds have him thinking like an ostrich. Sticking his head in the sand isn't an option. For beach, they'd have to walk a few blocks. There's no turning back, he must face this pack of people with a lion's bravery.

"So are we doing this?" chimes Reva's mom through a show of teeth. Weary and jetlagged, these parents need an injection of enthusiasm to compliment their caffeinated beverages.

Stella's mom, Lauren, Sam's dad, Rei, and Ant's dad, Luke, try to forge happy expressions from their malaise. But a half-glance across the street at a cosplayer mob is all it takes to turn their fake smiles upside down.

"Thought there'd be more dudes dressed up like HOAP," says Luke, fascinated by a middle-aged masked man with a big gut stretching the *H* on the chest of HOAP's classic patriotic getup.

Athleticism runs in Ant's family. If there were any sports fans around (there aren't), Luke might get mistaken for a retired wide receiver. Back home, they call Nay "Pocket Hercules" in reference to the former Mr. Universe who, at only 4'11", could bend steel bars with his bare hands.

"HOAP hasn't been cool for a while, Dad," says Ant, coming out of his meditation and turning around simultaneously. "He put the Fiendish Four in his cells like seven years ago. Hasn't done crap since."

"He's a meme," says Stella. "A joke. That guy is totally cosplaying him ironically."

The HOAP cosplayer even has a knockoff utility belt with a set of Pocket Protectors clipped end to end, going for max authenticity.

"Who's to say he wasn't in cahoots with the Fien

Four all along?" adds Sam, talking over his shoulder to the parents. "Out for his fifteen minutes of fame. … I bet TB3 Toys wishes they hadn't sponsored his little utility belt. Might've blew a chance to make Pocket Protectors cool again."

Reva taps her toes on the concrete. And immediately she senses her mom's concern, hotter on her neck than the sun. Amy's hyperaware when it comes to Reva's nervous tics. Talk of HOAP and the Fiendish Four always triggers her anxiety. Surfaces emotions about James's disappearance. And Reva will never give up the belief that the events are related.

"We better get going!" Amy exclaims. She's a mom on a mission to make this trip fun. Reva's ear-to-ear smile is fading fast and requires revival STAT. "Don't wanna miss the start of that nana-tech panel."

"It's nan-*o*-tech," snoots Sam. "Nana-tech, what is that, grandma technology?"

Reva fires Sam a look that says: *My mom isn't fodder for your noob-shaming.*

The tapping. Stella's no stranger to spikes in Reva's compulsive behavior. Reva has an autoimmune disorder called PANDAS. When she gets sick, the part of her body that fights off the infection makes her anxiety go haywire. Sometimes so badly, she becomes a different person and struggles to cope with activities that are normally trouble-free.

"*Protectors: Constellation Wars Part 2* world premiere," singsongs Stella, giving her best friend's arm a nudge. "T minus one hour."

This knack Stella has for tone and timing—Reva hopes she never loses it. Plus Stella always comes correct with the appropriate perspective. They're about to see never-before-seen footage of the upcoming

Protectors sequel. Why should some fat guy in a bad HOAP costume ruin the day?

"In case you come across a cool shirt or something," Amy whispers to Reva, slipping a twenty into the pocket of Reva's shorts.

Nothing like cold hard cash (and the bestest school friend and mom combo) to swing a mood back in the right direction. Reva's thoughts are off her dad and squarely on this newfound wealth. What to spend it on? Twenty bucks is four comics or a tee or an action figure.

Finally, the cars driven by adults in capes and the vans from various media outlets slow to a stop. The walk sign lights orange and all at once the street is animated. Sneakers and flip-flops united in the same direction. For a common cause. Gloriously nerdy crosstalk pushes the leftover bad vibes Reva got from the HOAP cosplayer to the far corners of her brain. It's heaven. Has to be. Walking straight into an all-inclusive Clash Comics Club would make any young reader feel this way.

"Heard a rumor that Julioception developed a *seventh* sense." ... "Because the wormhole sucked up all the star constellations!" ... "He amplified that guy's talent to fool lie detectors." ... "I mean, Agent Real-Estate dropped a house on her sister." ... "You can ask Orpha Mabe why Re-Lo did nothing, just don't expect an answer." ...

An Orpha Mabe mention turns Reva's head. The skinny guy in the snapback Protectors hat said it. He gives a nod to Reva's tee, detecting her shared affinity for Orpha Mabe, writer of the current Re-Lo run. Quickly, Reva spins to face the Convention Center again, hoping her mom doesn't catch her blushing (of course Amy does).

The talk that's on the tip of every nerd's tongue is the mystery supervillain. Beginning this year, Clash Comics plans to reveal a new villain as a Comic-Con tradition. For months, the silhouetted bad guy has been teased on the back pages of Protector comics. Today, he or she will at last be unveiled. Speculation in the streets ranges from a woman who can control gravity to a dude who can turn people into objects.

On the flight from Boston, Amy spoke of an era when nerdom wasn't as celebrated. Popular meant you were an athlete or cheerleader and liking video games or comics got you stuffed in a locker. James got his fair share of wedgies, peppered with spitballs, and accused of wearing a pocket protector. Not the collectible clip-on action figures, the plastic sleeve for holding pens in a shirt pocket. Doesn't matter that he didn't own one, back then it was part and parcel of the nerd stereotype.

As fan theories fly and friendly debates rage on, Reva sees the moral of Amy's story: It's a great day—a great birthday—to be a nerd at Comic-Con.

6
LOCATION, LOCATION, LOCATION

Reva's phone glows; she's just checking the time in the dark theater. The "Nanotechnology in Sci-Fi: Fact or Fiction" presentation has been babbling on for twenty minutes. Feels more like three hundred. Sam is absorbing every word from the panel. Furiously tapping notes for a future blog post. A look down the row of padded seats says it all: no one in their group gives two cares whether nanotechnology is fact or fiction. Amy's version, "nana-tech," would be much more interesting. Picturing a panel of nanas and grannies on stage discussing the latest Tupperware and heating pads makes Reva laugh out loud.

Stella has fallen asleep. And the parents—except for Reva's mom—aren't far behind. Reva misses the immersion of comic book culture that she got in the street. It isn't fair, being stuck in this boring talk. Outside, she was in the mix—she belonged. Forty more minutes of this will be torture. Catching some z's is out of the question with her adrenaline pumping so hard.

Reva gets an idea; she can fib about needing to use the bathroom. Organizing a walkout would ruin Sam's fun. His adrenaline levels might actually be higher, as the director of the most recent *Minuscule Molequle* movie discusses the nanotech in the character's suit at length;

and how we could use the tech someday for real. A bathroom trip is perfect. A few minutes alone on the show floor is what she needs—to breathe it all in.

"Bathroom," Reva whispers over Stella's sleeping body to Amy, four seats away. Amy checks that Reva has her phone, then gives the okay. It doesn't take Reva long to scoot out of the row and theater altogether. A blink and she's back in the buzz she was craving.

Reva drifts aimlessly into the crowd, ignoring the signs for the restrooms. There isn't a foot of show floor that isn't occupied by either a cosplayer or someone in superhero apparel.

"Whoops!" Reva steps on the back of a guy's skateboarder sneaks; she had been distracted by a woman's purple-and-yellow scaled power suit—Captain Clash! "Sorry," she says to the bearded man, who forgives and forgets at first sight of her Re-Lo tee.

Reva is carried past the mini-booths like a fish caught in a geeking current. She catches bits and pieces of things she missed while stuck in the nanotech presentation. Everyone is on his or her phone. What are they texting and video chatting about? Phase 3 of the C3U was announced? A Re-Lo solo film? It's about time! *Please be based off the Orpha Mabe run*, hopes Reva. *Who is playing Re-Lo, I wonder?*

As the name crosses Reva's mind, she looks up to see the eccentric fifty-nine-year-old creator, Orpha Mabe, in the flesh; burgundy hair and lipstick; big toothy smile; black tank, patterned skirt, vintage necklace. It's Orpha Mabe all right. Mabe is surrounded by handlers at a small table in front of the TB3 Toys booth. The TB3 Toys logo is very familiar to Reva; it's the company that made Pocket Protectors and the Pocket Protectors Palace Playset. TB3 Toys is the abbreviation for the company's full, tongue-twisting name, Toy Boat Toy Boat Toy Boat Toys. As for "Orpha Mabe," every real comic book fan knows it's a pen name to hide the fact that she's the daughter of Nell Sloan, writer of the first Re-Lo run in 1941.

Seeing Orpha Mabe will be the best thing Reva sees over the next three days at Comic-Con. Or maybe … not. Just beyond her favorite creator, she spots a counter displaying action figures and posable models, and amongst the rows and rows, a Re-Lo Pocket Protector with the color-changing bands that spiral down and around the arms of her black catsuit. The exact one that had vanished! … Except it doesn't have a smeared left eye. Never has Reva seen a Re-Lo for sale in person; it's been out of production since long before she was born. It's on eBay, but her mom still doesn't let her shop online.

The $20 Reva was given from her mom is burning a hole in her shorts pocket. It will take the whole amount to score the rare 3in figure; TB3 Toys won't be haggling. In her estimation, this Re-Lo is worth a thousand times that price tag. It was her dad's favorite Pocket Protector. Hers too. Even though Reva was five when it happened, she'll never forget how the Re-Lo with the smeared left eye mysteriously vanished. And left James's passed-down present incomplete.

There's only the one Re-Lo—she can't take the chance of losing out on it. Looking over her shoulder, Reva figures she's got time to buy it before a line forms for Orpha Mabe. She jumps to the counter, waving the twenty-dollar bill as a way of flagging down a worker.

"Good choice," says the TB3 Toys guy behind the register. "Not too many of these out there. … This one's in good shape."

When given her change and asked if she'd like a bag, Reva answers simply, "No." She clips the thumb-size action figure on her pocket straightaway. For all to see. It touched her skin briefly, but long enough to turn the spiral mood bands pink for *very happy*.

"Be sure to have Orpha Mabe sign something," adds the TB3 Toys guy. "Guessing you know she's Nell Sloan's daughter. You know, by your shirt and … taste in classic toys."

"Yeah," says Reva, face turning a shade off from Re-Lo's scarlet hair.

Speaking of Orpha Mabe, the line to meet her is forming fast. Guilt is weighing on Reva for having fibbed about needing to use the bathroom. At present, she's been apart from her group for longer than a typical pee break (or number two). If she doesn't return soon, her mom's going to freak—if she isn't freaking already. A round trip to the theater and back, and word will be out. The line for Orpha Mabe will be ridiculous. Never will she be this close to one of the industry's best creators again. She could appeal to her mom's soft side in a text with a string of heart emojis. But then her mom would know that she had lied. Peeing on her own would be strictly prohibited until her eighteenth birthday. … Or maybe, she could double down on the fib—say there's a super long line for the stalls. It's very believable. Most likely the truth. Plus, heart emojis.

Done. The text is off. It should buy Reva enough time to meet Orpha Mabe. Living with herself for lying gets easier with every person that double takes and then joins the wait. Mabe's signing prints of variant covers for *Re-Lo Kate Reborn #21: Location, Location, Location*. This is a relief to Reva because she doesn't have anything that could be autographed other than her tee.

The line moves pretty fast. Soon, it's the bearded guy in the skateboarder sneaks Reva stepped on, then her. Nervously, she kicks at the floor, contemplating things she could say: *You're my favorite writer. … Your writing is a big influence on mine. … My dad was a big fan of your dad. … In a way, I love comics because of both our dads.*

While Reva debates whether or not to speak (*Are you involved with the Re-Lo movie?*), her wandering eyes land on the HOAP cosplayer—the round man in the strained patriotic spandex. Miraculously, the costume is still held together by the red utility belt lined with Pocket Protectors. He smiles a self-deprecating smile at her. Stella was right; the man in the HOAP mask isn't serious, just out for laughs at the expense of the has-been hero. It's funny because it's exactly how an out-of-shape HOAP would look after all these years of inactivity, if he were to ever suit up again.

"Name? … Miss?"

At the moment, Reva's not home. She's lost inside a "daymare" where couch potato HOAP is stuffing his face with Funyuns and crying Mountain Dew tears while binge-watching old news footage and talk show appearances.

"Hello? … Earth to the girl who sorta looks like Re-Lo. …"

How embarrassing! Reva is holding everything up. Making Orpha Mabe wait! Quickly, she spins around to find Orpha Mabe staring at her with pen in hand.

"Re-Re-Reva. …" The sentiments Reva considered sharing, about Orpha being an influence and her dad being a fan—those are out the window. Reva's lucky she can squeak out her own name.

Naturally, the quick-witted Orpha Mabe signs:

30

To Re-Re-Reva,
I re-re-really like your
Re-Re-Re-Lo shirt.

– Orpha Mabe

As Orpha Mabe scribbles the message across a picture of Agent Real-Estate hurling a house at Re-Lo, Reva has an even scarier thought: she'll have to explain how she got it. Running into the Re-Lo writer in the women's room is a story that wouldn't hold water. Reva has no choice. She must come clean. And that's going to make the rest of the three days at the conference very restrictive.

Maybe it's the thought of facing Amy after lying to her. Or maybe, it's something Reva ate? Whatever it may be, Reva feels strange all of a sudden—as if she's being hugged. But no one is doing that.

"Here ya go," says Mabe, holding out the signed variant.

But Reva doesn't take the comic book cover. Because she can't. Her arms are at her side, unable to move. Mild discomfort skips straight to excruciating pain. A tube of toothpaste getting squeezed by a heavy hand—that's how she would describe her symptoms if a doctor were in the house. She can't feel her bones. Can't feel her weight. Inexplicably, she remains upright. Staring wide-eyed into an infinite bright light. The crowd, she fears, must see her as a two-dimensional object, stood in front of the TB3 Toys booth like a roll up banner.

A deafening hum drowns the hubbub and commotion. Reva wants to cup her ears in the worst way. Whatever is doing the squeezing coils around what's left of her insides and tightens its strangle. If she could, she would scream.

Then, as quickly as these wicked inflictions came over her, they exit in a mighty exhale. When Reva catches her breath, she finds herself in one piece—in one, three-dimensional piece. Only now, she is in a completely different location.

7
WHERE IS HERE?

"Dad?" gasps Reva.

Eight years. That's how long it's been. Could this really be her long-lost dad? He looks the same, like her. Apart from the deeper lines around his blue-green eyes and patches of white hairs on his bushy chin (last he saw Reva was also last he saw a beard trimmer apparently).

"Reva," breathes James. There is oddly no surprise in his quiet intensity, as if he had been expecting her.

Tears well in her eyes. She wonders if this is some cruel dream from which she can't wake. Dreams come about her dad often, but in the dreams his voice is never how she remembers it, how it sounds here. And never in these dreams does he appear any older than the age she knew him.

So maybe this *is* James standing before her. But why is he wearing a TB3 Toys tee shirt and track pants? Reva reaches to touch him. Because that could help answer the question. Her fingers jam against a clear barrier that wasn't so—painfully—obvious at first. Another detail she missed: the men suited in red-white-and-blue carbon fiber, circling her with baton weapons at the ready—sparks spitting from the tips, set to zap.

Fear would paralyze Reva if shock hadn't already.

Winding up here, face to face with her dad really did it to her. Not to mention the whole tube-of-toothpaste episode. She feels a little pee trickle out just thinking about it. Could be potentially helpful in the case of a return trip to Comic-Con; evidence that the bathroom lines were super long.

"They're not going to hurt you," says James, looking past Reva with eyes that seek mercy from whatever presence is over her shoulder.

Reva spins around. The sudden movement excites the henchmen along with their stun batons. She stops with her nose pressed into a giant American flag beach ball, or so it appears.

"At ease," booms a man's voice from above the "beach ball." The excited henchmen snap right to what was demanded of them, no questions asked. Next, a human hand reaches out from the beach ball and plucks the Re-Lo Pocket Protector from Reva's shorts.

Reva whips her attention back on James in search of answers. But her dad doesn't dare speak.

"You've had your fun," booms the voice, "but this one's mine now."

The voice doesn't make any sense. If he means the Re-Lo action figure, no fun was had with it. None at all actually. Reva just bought it a few minutes ago.

"To prove that I'm a man of my word, I'll let you keep this other one."

An identical Re-Lo Pocket Protector is tossed to Reva, which she catches with two hands. She's so confused. Why does swapping Re-Los make him "a man of his word"?

"Told you I wasn't heartless."

When did he tell me that? wonders Reva.

Reva shoves the figure down into her pocket,

blinking hard up at the beach ball that's finally coming into focus. It's the HOAP cosplayer from Comic-Con.

Until this moment, Reva hadn't observed the *here* in which she now exists. Anyone in the world would recognize this space immediately. Anyone not distracted by seeing her dad for the first time in eight years, after everyone presumed him gone. Walls are paneled with large gray tiles, floors are warm hardwood, and the lighting is white and bright. And glass. So much glass. The focal point, though, has to be the four customized cells that imprison the Fiendish Four. No mistaking it, this is HOAP's cellblock.

The smoked-filled cell still keeps Misbeehive calm. The narrow cell still restricts even the slightest movement from a deflated Bombastic. The tinted two-way-glass cell still holds a cracked Hoodwinker, who mumbles nonsensically. And the sub-zero cell still keeps the fire-pirate, *Arrr*son, on ice.

Reva looks up for the camera that flicked off when the livestream stopped getting hits. When people stopped caring about the Fiendish Four and resumed their everyday routines. She imagines its view panning back and forth. Recalls watching the Fiendish Four in their special cells with her mom. Hoping her dad would miraculously drop in like the villains had. As it turns out, James was here all along, in the cell next to *Arrr*son. Mere feet from being seen on camera.

Much of the cosplayer's face is masked with blue spandex. Uncanny, how his exposed facial features resemble HOAP's from seven years ago—when his mug was synonymous with *world hero*. Minus the scowl that he gives her for staring. That hawk nose—so close, Reva could touch it. There's hardly a laugh line. Might this be the real HOAP? It's certainly no HOAP

Halloween mask he's wearing. If indeed this is the real McCoy, every cent he earned in his fifteen minutes was spent on a boatload of plastic surgery. Who else could it be, but the real HOAP? The location of HOAP's secret headquarters has forever remained secret. If Reva's gut is correct, it means that the cosplayer is no cosplayer.

So many questions. How did she get here? How is it James is here—and why? Exactly *where* is here? Who are these henchmen? Why are there more empty cells beyond her dad's—and others that appear to be under construction? Why is HOAP still wearing Pocket Protectors?

Up close, Reva counts the five main Protectors around HOAP's belt, plus one she hadn't noticed before. She recognizes the action figure with the capsule-shaped helmet, node-laden power suit, and energy wrist-rings; he's a villain named Time Cap. Sparking through HOAP's popped neck veins is the same red lightning that once signalized villainy in the Fiendish Four.

Acting on HOAP's command, a couple of armored henchmen surround Reva. Stun batons fully charged. They grip her arms with their cold, carbon fiber fingers—then mechanically toss James a new cellmate.

What the heck? HOAP is supposed to be a good guy. The quick change from Comic-Con birthday girl to prisoner in HOAP's cellblock has thrown Reva completely off balance. Literally. As the auto-locking door seals her in, she whispers a Hail Mary birthday wish to catch the rest of that nanotech presentation.

8
TAL5

"Reva!" James didn't think HOAP and his henchmen would ever leave. At last, the cellblock is free of spandex and carbon fiber. Except for certain parts of the Fiendish Fours' costumes. But the weakened villains can't so much as stand; they don't really count.

James badly wants to give Reva a hug. But he can tell she needs answers, not affection. In the blink of an eye, she was here. Hard to blame her for doubting his identity.

"I'm sorry. ..." starts James, giving her space. "You must be so confused. ... Okay, let me see. ... Where to begin? ... You're in HOAP's headquarters. I'm assuming you've heard of him." James pauses to marvel at the remarkable girl who was pronouncing *hamburger* as *hamdurgver* when she last filled him with such wonder. "... My gosh, how old are you now? ... Twelve? Thirteen?"

"Twelve," murmurs Reva, quivering. "... I'm twelve today."

"Ohmigod. ... It's your birthday. ... Twelve, so ... eight years. I've been here eight years. To the day. ... For what it's worth, happy birthday."

In her heart, Reva had always detected that somehow everything was connected—her dad, the

Fiendish Four, HOAP, the vanishing Re-Lo. She wasn't crazy. She was right. It means that James was HOAP's first prisoner. A year ahead of *Arrr*son and the others. Feeling uneasy, Reva retreats mindlessly into the clear sidewall, banging her head on the glass.

"Are you okay?" James matches her grimace with one of his own, as if he also feels the throbbing. Deepening his focus beyond Reva, it strikes him how terrifying a cellblock of supervillains must be for a newcomer. "I'm not one of *them*," he reassures her while keeping his distance.

Turning, Reva has a direct view into *Arrr*son's subarctic cell. She could tap at him like a fish in a fishbowl if it weren't for the barrier her body is pressed against. *Arrr*son lies face down on the white floor, a low heat emitting from his shabby crimson pirate getup. He's alive. Barely.

"Maybe I can better explain," hails a boy's voice from the cell following theirs. It gives Reva yet another turn; she had assumed that the extra cells were vacant.

Judging by James's reaction—or lack thereof—he's familiar with the small, boyish figure that is speaking. Must be a fellow inmate.

The skinny boy appears to be near Reva's age. He has short dark hair, bright blue eyes, and a hawk nose. Outfit consists of an unzipped gray hoodie over (what else?) a TB3 Toys logo tee, and sweatpants that are ripped at the cuffs.

His cell is identical to James's; there's a slab bed, a sink, and a toilet in the back corner. After careful study, Reva spots a cylindrical pedestal that her dad's cell doesn't include. A battery pictogram on the digital screen hints that it could be a charging station of sorts.

Reva holds her breath as the boy comes to the

closest wall of his cell. "HOAP is my grandfather," he says, loud enough to reach her ears through the thick glass. "You'd never guess it, but he's actually eighty years old. Kid you not. In 1976, he discovered something that no one else has. Even to this day. A substance. In the ground. He stopped aging the second it made contact. ..."

Similar to James, this boy gives Reva the impression that he is well adjusted to his conditions. "... The substance can bring ideas to life. Any idea that's embodied in a tangible item—like an action figure. ... Or a Pocket Protector."

She can't decide whether to keep listening or stick a finger in each ear.

"HOAP's alter ego is Tal Boatwright III," the boy goes on. "Former editor-in-chief of Clash Comics. Founder of TB3 Toys. Fans shortened it to TB3. If you're into comics, you've heard of him. TB3's best known for his underground fiction. Last public sighting was in '86. ... The fans are right. He's the writing credit that Clash blacks out on the covers. HOAP's a bad dude. Not the hero everyone thinks he is. Locked me here—his own grandson—because of what I know!"

According to James's expression, the boy is telling the truth. But can Reva really believe that this guy is actually her dad? He could easily be some nutjob. There's also the possibility that some jerk at Comic-Con slipped her a mind-altering drug. Maybe she's been reading too many comic books. Or maybe not.

"I see that you are 73.2% skeptical, Reva," the boy says with a straight face.

"I've never even met you," she says, fidgeting. "How do you know my name?"

"My name is Tal," states the boy. "The fifth. Tal

Boatwright V. But you can call me Tal5. ... I've been here to witness countless acts of TB3's wickedness. Experienced his capacity for evil firsthand. ... Could let you see for yourself if only you had a Re-Lo."

Without realizing it, Reva's hand slides over the pocket of her shorts. The cat that swallowed the canary; Tal5's led a sheltered life but the saying isn't foreign to him. He made the association as soon as Reva showed that self-satisfied smirk. She *does* have a Re-Lo. "Don't let him see it," warns Tal5, low enough not to arouse *Arrr*son's suspicions.

Tal5 contains his excitement. The security camera watching their cells can't catch sight of anything unusual or it could bring trouble. "Act casual," he says.

"Act casual?" snaps Reva. *How is that even remotely possible?*

"Slowly take your hand off your pocket," says Tal5 without moving his lips. "That Pocket Protector is our ticket out of here. The henchmen will be back for it in seconds if you're not discreet."

"HOAP knows I have it," asserts Reva. "He swapped it with the one I bought at Comic-Con. Didn't you see?"

"I was ... sleeping at the time," Tal5 mutters.

James is thinking what Tal5 is thinking, as if a light just flicked on inside his head. It makes Reva drop her arms, you know, "act casual." They've managed to convince her in part that the Re-Lo is, somehow, a valid means of escaping.

"The Re-Lo in my pocket ... is that what brought me here?" asks Reva with one eye on the security cam.

"HOAP did," says Tal5. "He casts Pocket Protectors from the substance. That's where he gets his powers. From the action figures. The Re-Lo on his belt gives him the power to people-shift."

"What good is this one then?" she questions. "I don't feel any superpowers. And why would HOAP give me superpowers?"

"The one you have isn't cast from the substance," assures Tal5. "He keeps that collection well guarded. When not on his belt, they're sealed away in the control room. Just once has someone—" That last line seemed to slip out with a very suspicious side-glance at James.

"What does *that* mean?" asks Reva to both.

"HOAP must have forgotten what *James*—" James quickly edits himself—"what *I* used for a catalyst in Tal5."

Reva doesn't follow.

"Tal5 can make it so you understand everything," says James. "… Bravery is in his code."

Reva shows her hands how a traffic cop would to stop cars coming from both directions. "Wait," she whispers. "Catalyst. Code. A charging station. Tal5, are you some kind of a—"

"You don't have to whisper," Tal5 interrupts. "There are no listening devices. We're alone most of the time. Nothing much to say. … Nothing worth saying. … And the four fiends over there are well aware of my deal. What I'm trying to say, Reva, is, yes, your assumption is 100% correct. I am some kind of a robot."

There's nothing that Reva is a hundred percent sure about at the moment, except that her head is spinning.

"I've run the simulations," says Tal5. "Calculated the probabilities. We get one shot at this."

"Shot at what?" says Reva.

"Giving you Re-Lo's powers," says Tal5.

"I'm not saying I believe you—because I like, 95%

don't—but let's for a second imagine that Pocket Protectors can give people powers. And I can become Re-Lo. Have you accounted for HOAP? From what I gathered, he can be every Protector combined—plus Re-Lo's archvillain, Time Cap. With Julioception, he'd see the move coming a mile away. If he hasn't already. I won't stand a chance."

"First, you 99.9% don't believe me," says Tal5. "Let's be honest. ... Second, you're absolutely right. You wouldn't stand a chance against HOAP. Truth is, the only way out of this prison is backward."

"*Resurgent Re-Lo #45*," says James, "*Revisionist's History.*"

James's comic collection is stored in boxes under Reva's bed; she's read the *Revisionist's History* storyline a billion times. *Maybe this IS my dad*, she thinks, regarding him from a new angle. In hindsight, James should have led with comics. His ginger coloring and blue-green eyes sure are convincing when he's making obscure Re-Lo references. The fact that James can connect with his daughter through a comic book title that's four decades old turns up the corners of his mouth—facial muscles he hasn't exercised in a long, long while.

"Revisionist rewrites the president's history," says Reva. "Turns her evil. So Re-Lo investigates the alternate timeline for a way to course-correct the future." By the end of Reva's recap, James's smile has stretched to his ears.

"You think breaking down TB3's past can break us out of here," she concludes. "But what would stop me from shifting my dad to an army of tanks that could scare the pants off HOAP if he followed?"

"Electromagnetic shielding," states Tal5. "The electromagnetic shielding would stop you. It's conductive—the glass. To guard against incoming and—in our case—outgoing emissions of electromagnetic waves."

"Dang," sighs Reva, giving the clear walls a once-over. Any hardcore Re-Lo fan could spell out the noteworthiness of the defense measure: electromagnetic shielding prevents location-shifts.

"These cells were constructed over a span of thirty years," says Tal5. "TB3 thought of absolutely everything."

"There's no electromagnetic shield between here and days gone," says James.

"But you said so yourself," Reva counters in Tal5's direction, "you've been here all along. What could I possibly learn about this place that you don't already know? What part of TB3's history could possibly get us out of here?"

"Where we are," answers James, "on the map. With that information alone, Si Q could—"

"Si Q?" grills Reva. "Where are we gonna get a Si Q?"

"There's a way," assures Tal5. "HOAP's origin story. We've been told much of it. But there are gaps. Most crucially, why did TB3 do it? Understanding his motivation could uncover a weakness. Reveal a pattern. Point to an opportune time to strip him of his powers."

"Get Si Q on a pocket of someone worthy," inserts James. "Supplied with our whereabouts, that person could release the locks on these doors."

"And the locks on the Pocket Protector units," states Tal5. "We could end him."

Reva entertains this madness solely because it's got the backing of her cellmate, who she's beginning to accept as her real dad. She doesn't have a computer brain like Tal5 claims to have under his parted hair, but she has a heart that she trusts. A good twenty percent of her is still fretting that James is an actor or imposter … or a hallucination. Might there have been a Fig-Mental cosplayer at Comic-Con messing around with an actual fear toxin? If foul play is involved, someone will surely rot in jail when this draws to a close.

"And what if I do discover something?" she says. "That can save us. There'd be nothing we could do about it from here."

"Well, that's why you're the only one here who can be Re-Lo," says Tal5. "None of us have a spiritual link to anyone on the outside."

9
TIME TO RELOCATE!

"SpaceTime!" In early comics, the contrivance Re-Lo utilized to video chat through space and time was called a Comm-Rift. After smartphones became a thing, it was renamed to play off Apple's FaceTime. "... I could open a direct video line to the authorities. Tell them we're in HOAP's cellblock."

"Do you share a spiritual link with a detective?" asks James. "Did your mom remarry? No—don't tell me. I don't want to know."

What kind of Re-Lo reader is Reva? An absentminded one, she'd say. Re-Lo can only SpaceTime with her main contacts—her fellow Protectors, for example; that's like, Re-Lo 101. It's super embarrassing to stump on a detail such as this in front of her dad. If it weren't for the whole captivity thing, he'd be president of the Re-Lo fan club.

"Then I'll SpaceTime with Mom," responds Reva. "Mom can alert the authorities."

"Ripping open a rift in space and time would bring every henchmen HOAP's got," warns Tal5, mindful of the security camera. "They'd be on top of us before you could get your mom to listen. Plan to link with someone who wouldn't be fazed by the fantastical yarn you'll be spinning. Someone with the grit to get in the way of his new scheme."

"I can think of a few peeps who might fit that description," says Reva.

"Had a chance once to learn where in the world we are exactly," says Tal5, "but a single blink depleted my battery. … According to my calculations, there's equal chance we're either under the sea or over the clouds."

"I can't do this by myself," murmurs Reva. "Dad— if you are my dad—you'll come with me, right?"

James views the white floor. "Even if we had two Re-Los … I can't experience it again. It has to be you. Tal5's right. You're the only one who can get the message out."

"What about Mom?" says Reva. "There has to be a spiritual connection between you still."

"… I don't know. …" James contemplates the floor some more.

"Wait," says Reva, jerking her head at Tal5. "What was all that you said about a new scheme?" Reva's reaction time had been delayed between her butterflies and the wishful thoughts of a family reunion.

"He put on an addition," quips Tal5. "We believe he's expanding his rogues' gallery. And that it's related to Clash's villain rollout. New baddie every year. … Cell next to mine has crystal walls. Designed to contain whatever it is the next guy or girl can do. … We recognize this much about HOAP's motivation—he can't stand being irrelevant. A joke. A has-been. Reality shows don't even ring him."

Tal5 points straight through Reva's cell to the custom holdings for *Arrr*son, Hoodwinker, Bombastic, and Misbeehive. "They were innocent once. TB3 used them. Robbed them of lives. Took them from their families. Once a villain Pocket Protector takes hold …"

He lets the Fiendish Four's diminished state complete his point. "If you don't do this, more people like them will suffer. But we need to know when—and who—he plans to strike."

"Where are we gonna get this … 'substance'?" By Reva's evaluation, the toilet in Tal5's cell is the lone spot that could keep a substance. Because robots don't need toilets, right? "If it involves your toilet, I'm out. Just sayin'."

Tal5 throws his hoodie off his shoulders. *Odd answer to my question*, Reva thinks. Then he takes a powerful grip of his left forearm, just below the elbow. He does it while staring at Reva through the cell walls. Deep breaths. A series of them. How a human would take in air before a dangerous stunt.

"Time to relocate!" cries Tal5, wrenching his forearm clockwise. In the next motion, he rips it clear from the elbow socket.

The detached limb smacks the smooth floor. Reva is horrorstruck. Blood, the color blue, hemorrhages from Tal5's elbow like a malfunctioning water sprinkler.

Where muscles and ligaments should be (relative to the mannequin in Reva's health class), there are gears, motors, and shredded strands of synthetic fiber.

What's stranger, Tal5 doesn't appear to be in any pain. *Thrilled*, as it happens, is how Reva would describe his mood. It's beyond her why anyone would relish drowning in something like one hundred pens exploding ink. "It's blue!" cackles Tal5. "It's blue!"

"Aaand why is blue good?" Reva questions.

Tal5 plugs his open elbow "wound" with the hand that remains attached. "The red lightning. The streaks in TB3's veins. In theirs." (He can't do more than nod in the Fiendish Four's direction.) "It's merely a theory, but I think a living being using the substance for good can—over time—develop the power to destroy it altogether. Blue means good. Blue means we have a chance!"

Reva swings her attention to James—calm, cool, collected James, the robotics engineer, who apparently is conditioned to robots acting the fool. "I thought you were putting me on! He's actually a robot? And you knew he was filled with this … stuff? … Wait. … Did you make Tal5?"

Instructions that Tal5 barks hit Reva's ears before James can reply.

"While you're in the past, time stops for you here!" Blue substance is spurting between Tal5's fingers. "You might only get a few seconds to SpaceTime when you return! So make it count!"

"Are you ready?" mumbles James. It was practically another life, but she remembers her dad having the gift of gab. He must have lost the gift in this isolation.

"Is this really real?" asks Reva. The nanotech presentation was a snoozefest. Maybe she never left it. Zonked out with the others in the cushiony theater seats. Any second now she could awaken, safe and sound next to Stella.

James nods in response to Reva's question. Of course he does. Dreams will have you believing they're real right up until they're not. The level of crazy doesn't matter. Reva couldn't say whether she's really asleep or really awake with any real confidence. All she knows is that things just got real.

HOAP's suited squad swarms the cellblock in a rush of patriotic colors. Tal5's synthetic insides take the henchmen by surprise too; it's evident in the collective wide eyes over their face shields.

"Get him to the workshop!" shouts the ranking henchman.

One henchman uses the security keypad outside Tal5's cell. The rest enter when the door opens, stun batons raised.

The wall of Tal5's cell that faces Reva looks like someone splashed the glass with blue paint by the bucket load. Reva strains her eyes to follow the wild skirmish. From her obstructed vantage, Tal5's not putting up much of a fight. Two henchmen have Tal5 by his prosthetic shoulders. Next, they're dragging him into the corridor.

Reva isn't sure what to do. Tal5 didn't one hundred percent write out her task list. Whatever Tal5 hoped to pull off by pulling off a forearm, it can't be going as planned. Thick glass is thick glass—even if she had step-by-step instructions, her hands would be tied.

"The holes," says James. Along the front wall of the cell are fist-size ventilation holes in a line. Reva hadn't noticed until James pointed them out.

Giving the impression that a merciless paintball war recently took place, the paint-splattered henchmen clank across Reva's view with seize of Tal5, or in this analogy, the one-man blue army.

Reva reaches down into her pocket for the Re-Lo and makes a fist around it. This is all so insane … but she has to play it out. There aren't any other choices. None right under her nose, at least. And if she wakes suddenly, and this is but a dream, then how happy she will be to learn more about nanotech.

A disquieting mental picture comes over Reva: her cell is the gas tank, Tal5's spurting elbow is the nozzle, and the blue substance is the gas. And she's set to get a gallon's worth through one of the ventilation holes. It's no great consolation, but the exposed parts of the henchmen's faces are covered in the stuff and they appear to be okay. Their skin isn't melting or any such horror.

Contorting himself, Tal5 is able to make eye contact with Reva around the henchman on his arm. She gives a squeeze of the Re-Lo in her pocket anxiously; it would seem that it's go time. Tal5 maintains his grasp of the shredded veins in his elbow joint, holding back what substance he can.

Not another second can tick away; Tal5 squirms free from the henchman and dives for Reva's cell—inserting the gushing end of his amputated arm into a ventilation hole.

Reva lunges forward with Re-Lo out in her palm. Tal5's blood—his "catalyst"—sprays erratically into her cell, dousing the thumb-size action figure in the substance (along with everyone and everything). The pooled substance molds to the plastic and Reva's flesh with a visible mesh pattern. Almost instantly, she shows a faint presence of that "skin lightning." If Tal5's color theory is sound, then she's lucky that the streaks in her arm are blue, not villain-red.

Tal5's elbow pops out of the hole in the glass as the henchmen yank him back. Acting on instinct, Reva clips Re-Lo to the right-hand pocket of her shorts.

"Go now!" screams Tal5 as the henchmen swallow him up with their batons hammering away.

Reva wants nothing more than to do precisely that—"Go now!" But she has no idea where or—more accurately—*when* to go.

"It's just another case for the time detective," assures James, noticing that she has started tapping her toes—nervously, uncontrollably. "Think of the mystery you want solved, and Re-Lo's power will pull up the time scenes you need to see."

Tal5 is getting dragged off, showing the worse for wear after his efforts. No doubt the henchmen will return for her when they've dumped Tal5 in the scrap pile. She rolls her arm, watching a little blue lightning bolt zap under the sleeve of her Re-Lo tee. Trying new things, taking risks—not really her thing. But maybe the moment has finally come to change all that.

"Understanding TB3's motive is how we stop him," says James. "With that goal in mind you'll time-shift. You just be your observant self. … If you're anything like me, that is."

Observant is certainly one of Reva's strong suits. On the other hand, she's never time traveled or investigated a time scene before. And then there's this giant hurdle in front of her, this problematic anxiety. Getting to the bottom of HOAP's motivation might be trickier than she thinks— (As soon as she thinks, she blinks.)

10
WALK THIS WAY

Reva floats over a blue-and-white shag carpet in a bedroom, a boy's, if the decor and classic rock posters papering the walls are any indication. The room is dark, save for a sliver of moonlight shining through one of the windows.

"You'll be invisible! ..." James's voice is distant, reaching her from who knows how far off, from the cell in the present. "... A ghost. ..." The faintness tells Reva that she must have gone back a ways.

Re-Lo assumes the properties of a ghost when investigating scenes. Reva hadn't forgot, but she's glad to hear that her dad's looking out for her. He must have assumed that everything would be kind of a blur at first.

The blink here wasn't as painful as her displacement from Comic-Con to HOAP's cellblock. A static shock—like when you scuff your socks on the carpet and then touch metal—is a good comparable. This static shock, though, is one Reva feels from her head down to her feet. Getting snatched by a location-shifter is a thousand times worse, no question. Unless you enjoy having your body squashed like a ham-fisted brute's tube of toothpaste.

HOAP is solely to blame for her current whereabouts, or *when*abouts. That fact has been established. His motive for kidnapping her, locking her up, swiping the Re-Lo she bought at Comic-Con—that's what she's come back in time to discover.

In addition to the allover static shock, Reva feels the onset of a new nervous tic; she is compelled to keep checking her Pocket Protector, its tightness. Doesn't matter that her fingers repeatedly pass clear through her leg. As a comic book character, Re-Lo can't get stuck on a case such as this because … well, because she's Re-Lo. Reva's only Re-Lo because a Re-Lo action figure makes her Re-Lo. What if it comes off her pocket on a time-shift? It's weird enough being see-through.

A loud drumming noise suddenly puts Reva's anxious thoughts of being trapped in time-limbo on hold. And next thing she knows, she's recoiling through a bookshelf. She floats there, commingling with back issues of Clash comics. If her body had mass, the collection would be strewn about the carpet.

Reva glides out of the shelves to browse the front-facing covers; at a glance, the most recent issue is *The Planet's Proud Protectors #152*, which released in 1976, the year her dad was born.

These are classics. Worth a ton—if the entire collection weren't defaced. Someone drew mustaches on the faces of every character. Even Re-Lo and Ursa Double-Major have hairy upper lips. It makes Reva sick to her stomach.

The loud drumming happens again. This second session isn't as startling, which makes the tapping easier to discern. It's not stick on drumhead; it's fingers on wood. In all likelihood, they're the same fingers that took a fat marker to these comics. Reva arrived not too long ago, so this is the first she's scoping anything beyond the unmade bed. A seated boy—a seventh-grader by the looks of him—raps a desk to the rock and roll blaring from his jumbo headphones. These tan beauties are definitely not Beats by Dre. ... Hovering near, she's able to read the logo off the cushioned D-shaped ears. ... *Koss*. Kids from her time call these "retro."

The boy busily sketches in a drawing pad, pausing now and then to calculate his next line with more finger drumming. Reva gets a sense that she knows this boy from somewhere. That hawk nose, it's very familiar. When his face catches the lamplight, the mental block is lifted straightaway. This boy shares a striking resemblance with Tal5. Take scissors to his shoulder-length spiky shag hairdo and the pair could be twins.

Reva follows the wire from the retro headphones to a woodgrain record player with oversized silver knobs. She recognizes the wordmark, that goes round and round on the turntable, from the roller coaster at Disney World (the destination of her tenth birthday party with family in 2018). The music playing is a song by Aerosmith.

For a second while Reva was commingling with the comics, she wondered if this might be her dad's childhood bedroom. That theory died with the discovery of the drawn-on mustaches; it never would have been born if she had started with the full tour. James was a certified neat freak. At no age could he have lived with his floors in this state—a mess of crumpled paper balls, solid-color tees, and cuffed denim.

All of a sudden, the door to the shadowy bedroom swings open, allowing a cone of light in from the bright hallway. Reva—surprised again—lets out a gasp, but the boy and the person at the door can't hear it.

It's HOAP who stands where the blue-and-white shag joins a brown carpet. Technically it's HOAP's alter ego that Tal5 had spoiled back in the cellblock. Namely, Tal Boatwright III—TB3 for short—the underground comic book creator, former editor-in-chief of Clash Comics, and TB3 Toys founder.

At this range, Reva can totally picture TB3 with the HOAP mask on. In retrospect, his hawk nose is a dead giveaway. For "street clothes" he wears a beige vintage leisure jacket with pockets on each breast, jeans, and a collared shirt (three buttons undone to show off his hairy chest). The exclusion of a mask gets her a good description of his noggin; dark hair parted to one side, bushy sideburns, a chevron mustache, and aviator eyeglasses.

According to Tal5, TB3 hasn't aged since discovering the substance in 1976. Unless Tal5 had his facts wrong, this scene could be *any*time between 1976 and present day.

"Tal!" says TB3. The teen rocker is head down in his work while a shrieking guitar riff wails from the Koss ear cups. TB3 must repeat himself over and over while raising his volume to that of a shout.

The boy who could be Tal5's twin is also named Tal; that's been made abundantly clear. (Reva will regard him as just plain "Tal" with no number.) Tal knows full well that TB3 is standing in the sudden light source. By ignoring him, Tal's hoping he'll leave. More screams of Tal's name say that's not happening. So with a reddened face, Tal angrily rips off his headphones.

"I told you to knock, Dad!"

Reva needs a quick break to sort this out. A second ago, Tal identified TB3 as his dad. Back in the cell, Tal5 referred to TB3 as his grandfather. Which means the Tal in this scene is Tal Boatwright IV. … And, somehow, Tal5's father. (How a robot has a family lineage is yet another mystery for the pile of mysteries.)

"I didn't knock," retorts TB3, pushing on the rim of his massive, metal eyeglass frames, "because I knew you wouldn't hear me. That volume is going to ruin your ears."

"What do you care?" snaps Tal, diving back to his character shading.

Tal is penciling a comic panel. It's good. Really good. Like, he could draw for Clash Comics type of good. Reva catches TB3 admiring Tal's sketched heroes that descend on a flock of winged aliens.

"It's almost midnight," says TB3, hinting for Tal to call it a day.

"So?" Tal counters.

"So … it's a school night. And you need the grades if you plan to follow in my footsteps."

"Why would I ever want to do that?" Tal wishes he could take it back as his dad's face falls. "It's just … we never see you. … You're always working."

Sent into a spin, TB3's thoughts come out no less flustered, "I'm sorry, I … I didn't think you … I can be here—"

"Let me guess," mutters Tal, "there's a new character in the hallway."

TB3 hangs his head, guilty as charged.

"I'm not your son," resigns Tal. "I'm your personal focus group."

Tal's right. There's a poster board within TB3's reach, leaning against the doorjamb.

"Well? … Are you going to show me or not?"

As if being forced against his will, TB3 raises the

poster board into the borrowed light from the hall. It displays concept art for a character that is immediately familiar to Reva; a male character set apart by his trademark, capsule-shaped mask and a skinsuit studded with electrified nodes. TB3 has designed a villain, as conveyed in the artwork by a range of crooked expressions and nefarious poses.

"You've done it again," says Tal, scrutinizing the space-age bracelets, which appear to function as displays for vital graphical data. "More top-notch work by you. ... The kids you really care about will love it. Totally worth shutting Mom and me out for the next six months."

"You're not my focus group," TB3 says in a loving voice that fights back a cry. "You're my inspiration. I work hard so you'll be proud of me. Proud to be a Tal Boatwright. It might sound corny, but ... I want nothing more than to be your ... hero."

"You're right, it does sound corny," spits Tal. "If you're taking this opportunity to workshop a script, my suggestion would be to scrap that line. ..."

Reva can tell that Tal regrets being so mean—that until this very moment, he hasn't looked at the situation from TB3's point of view. Before this scene, Tal only saw a dad who cared more about the next comic or the next big thing to fly off toy shelves.

11
TIME CAP

"What's his name anyway?" Tal steals another glance at the node-laden character on the poster board leaning against his dad's leg. He tries to look more interested in his own sketch than TB3's polished concept art.

TB3 can't bottle his enthusiasm, flourishing the board. "Thought I'd call him Time Capsule—Time Cap for short."

"Stupid name," Tal fibs, unwilling to ditch the attitude just yet. "What's he do?"

"New Re-Lo villain," says TB3 as Tal's phony criticism rolls off his back. "These nodes allow him to store energy over time and release it in the present. Older the trap, stronger the blast. He can see possible futures—relay the visions to another's subconscious. Which basically means he can reshape time itself to his advantage. Time Cap is literally timeless—he doesn't age."

"Whatever," Tal says with a dismissive wave. Truth be told, Time Cap strikes Tal as a pretty dope character. But under no circumstances is he going to give TB3 the satisfaction of hearing that.

Reva is well up on Time Cap. He's been a recurring enemy of Re-Lo's since *Re-Lo Kate #228* (1977). Through the years he's made many appearances, taking on several different forms, but the artwork on the poster board depicts early Time Cap. All things considered, this scene must take place in 1976—the year Tal5 claims HOAP discovered the substance. If this is indeed the case, then Time Cap wouldn't strike Tal as a "pretty dope" character, it would strike him as a "far out" character.

Reva's read the first Time Cap arc a few times. It was in the box of old comics her dad left behind when he vanished. TB3 just explained the villain's abilities to Tal: Time Cap could store energy in the past and unleash it in the present—as fast as Re-Lo could location-shift. Fights between the two were fast and frenetic.

Time Cap tried time and again in those first ten issues to end the woman who stood between him and world domination. To neutralize Re-Lo's shift power, he cast electromagnetic fields in the form of invisible nets.

If the nets work for Time Cap in the comics, they must work for HOAP in real life, Reva deduces. *It's why he used them to keep Re-Lo people like me in and out of his cells.*

Re-Lo was almost done for in issue #237 when Si Q saved her at the last possible second by disabling the nets. A close call that led to the evolution of her shift ability. By shifting back in time, Re-Lo could pinpoint the placement of Time Cap's energy traps. But Time Cap had already seen a future where Re-Lo possessed this upgrade. To combat it, he stored energy everywhere and every*when*, dating back thousands—no, billions—of years. If detonated, that magnitude of amassed energy could have leveled the entire Eastern Seaboard.

Setting that many energy traps that far back in time expended every ounce of Time Cap's metaphysical energy—spiritual energy. As the story framed, people leave traceable records of every moment from their lives. These records are comprised entirely of spiritual energy, into which Re-Lo can shift.

Time Cap became distracted with ideas for his predestined rule. That's when Re-Lo chain-shifted across every trace of energy he left in time, scattering his records into harmless fragments. The awesome move drained Time Cap of his vitality and rendered him a weak, soulless being.

"I want you to have the prototype Time Cap." TB3's voice removes Reva from her vivid recall of the first Time Cap tale, the very one that its writer, TB3, as of this scene, has yet to tell. She watches TB3 relocate a 6in Time Cap action figure from the left breast pocket of his leisure jacket to Tal's desk.

"Put it with the others," Tal retorts with a toss of his shaggy hair.

TB3 takes Time Cap up to a shelf above Tal's workspace, finding five spots in a layer of dust where other action figures like it were once posed. The sight horrifies TB3. And also makes him sneeze.

Tal points TB3 to where the shelf's former contents currently reside: the trash bin on the floor.

"What the heck, Tal?" whines TB3, falling to his knees. "… Collectors would do anything for these!" Ever so carefully, TB3 fishes the precious action figures out of the discarded tissues, crumpled paper balls, and chewed gum. "… The rest of the world gets cheap plastic! You get one-of-a-kind prototypes."

TB3 cradles the 6in hand-painted action figures of

the five main Protectors into the light for a damage assessment. Craving the same attention to which his dad gives the toys, Tal kicks out his desk chair and then sweeps the new Time Cap figure off the dusty shelf. Down it falls into the trash bin with a *thud*.

"Tal, what are you doing?" TB3 rests the Protectors on Tal's rumpled bed sheets and wastes no time salvaging the prototype Time Cap from the waste. "You chipped one of his nodes!" he groans while fingering a minor nick on the character's skinsuit.

"You're pathetic!" Tal shouts, with an immediate want to make his feelings known through better words. "… You care more about a stupid node on a stupid toy than you care about me."

A broken heart, TB3 is reminded, hurts worse than a broken power node. Then TB3 spots on Tal's desk what he believes is, without question, the source of Tal's angst: a certificate for some award.

"The world thinks you're this amazing person," Tal continues, shuffling his illustrations on top of the certificate. "… I wish people knew the truth."

Reva didn't get a good look at it. Neither did TB3, but to him it's no mystery. "I missed your show. Ohmigod. It completely slipped my mind." A step taken by TB3 in Tal's direction, and the teen's drawing arm is on the stack of illustrations like a paperweight.

"You took first place, didn't you?"

"I wish I sucked at comics!" cries Tal, spinning in the chair to chuck a graphite pencil at the sloped wall over his bed.

It took TB3—and Reva—some reflection to interpret Tal's outburst. They read it as such: If TB3 didn't boast the talent that Tal inherited, then TB3 wouldn't be famous and gone all the time.

"You're right," says TB3.

Tal's shadowing of an alien's underbelly stops. A lecture is what he had been expecting, on TB3's importance to the comic and toy industries.

"I'll promote someone into my role. Starting tomorrow, I'm hands-off. ... Forgive me, Tal. For not recognizing it sooner. ... They can rewrite Re-Lo's reality so she's an agent of The Empusa for all I care. ... That's actually a decent idea ... maybe a villain called Revisionist is behind it ..." TB3 digresses for a second before remembering his new outlook ... "I'll pass it along and detach myself from it."

Tal does his very best to hide his approval and keep the corners of his mouth from curling up.

TB3 lays his leisure jacket across the bed and lines the six action figures on top of it. Before swaddling the prototypes in the polyester, he finally sees how Tal viewed them—as symbols of his excuses and feigned apologies.

Determined to change how Tal views him, TB3 rids his boy's bedroom of the action figures, carrying them out in the jacket under his arm.

Reva must follow. She phases straight through Tal, his desk, and the wall, to the brighter hallway, still amazed that she can do such a thing. Ahead of her, she spots TB3 turning down the staircase.

Like a gust of wind, she whisks after him with her feet sailing over the carpet. Down the stairs and through the foyer Reva pursues, then out the double entry doors into the front yard.

12
UNDER THE GOLDEN STATUE

In-ground lamps light TB3's hurried way along a stone path. The lawn which the path intersects is meticulously groomed and bordered by edged flowerbeds and sculpted shrubbery. Reva stays on TB3's heels, gliding through the cool midnight air. Nervousness about missing something vital to the mission makes Reva fidget with the invisible force emanating from Re-Lo, as a substitute for tapping her feet.

They're headed straight for a giant statue of a man reaching his right arm to the stars. Lit up with spotlights, this statue is the unmissable focal point of the grounds. Just as Reva puts it in her head that the almighty statue is TB3's destination, he stops short. Retaining the properties of a ghost, she passes directly through him.

In the green grass a few steps from the path lies the object that made TB3 heel brake like a cartoon character—a shovel.

"They left their tools again," mutters TB3.

Then TB3 has a bright idea, as though a spotlight from the statue ahead were suddenly pointed at the shovel. He plucks the tool off the ground with purpose, convinced that it had been left there specifically for his use at this exact moment. Before Reva can dash aside, TB3 is storming through her—shovel in one hand, bundle of action figures carried like a football in the other.

The statue they're moving closer to must be of a man that TB3 holds in the highest regard; Reva bases this assumption on its golden color and sheer enormity.

Soon she is at the foot of the golden statue, invisibly alongside TB3 who stands facing his mansion. He remains oblivious to the fact that she is there watching his every move.

Reva has to crook her neck way back for a view up the larger-than-life statue. The sculpted man has TB3's face—the hawk nose, large glasses, and chevron mustache—and is portrayed as a thirtysomething, TB3's ballpark age in this scene. Where TB3's hair is parted to the side, the statue man's hair is slicked back. Hairstyle notwithstanding, she is positive that the golden man has the names Tal and Boatwright printed on his birth certificate. As it happens, that detail is spot-on. Confirmed by that *spot on* the stone base where it's etched: Tal Boatwright Jr. Creator. Innovator. Hero.

This statue is of TB3's father, Reva concludes. *Founder of Clash Comics in 1939.*

"I tried to be you," TB3 says up at the statue, "but he doesn't want you. ... I have to become something else. ..."

TB3 lays out his leisure jacket on the grass, exposing the six nestled action figures to the moonlight (Re-Lo, Si Q, Ursa Double-Major, Julioception, Talent Master, and the conceptual villain at the time of this scene, Time Cap).

After rolling up the sleeves of his button-down shirt, TB3 grips the borrowed shovel with both hands.

"These figures are symbols of what a crappy dad I've been." TB3's immortalized father is, evidently, a very good listener. "I was going to drop them through a sewer grate or something. … But then this shovel was there. … Told me a proper burial was in order."

With aims to dig these action figures a grave, TB3 begins driving the blade through the sod and heaving scoop after scoop of rocks and dirt over his shoulder.

"You're probably thinking I'm not capable— nnnugh—of burying my past," grunts TB3 while loosening a boulder in the earth. "But I'm out to prove you wrong. From this moment forth—nnnugh—I'm a changed man. I will give these relics peaceful rest— nnnugh—so they will not haunt me!"

On the next downward thrust, the blade of the shovel gets stuck. TB3 can't pull the shovel out, hard as he tries. Even with his mightiest pull, the tool won't budge. Darkness shrouds the bottom of the hole, so what's down there is anybody's guess.

While Reva is taking a few educated guesses, she loses TB3 somewhere in the night's shadows. Fortunately, locating him doesn't require a tracker's keen senses—he's ripping up the nearest in-ground lamp and stretching the wire over to the dig site. The light uncovers a viscous substance—purple in color— flooding the three-foot hole from below the shovel blade.

"What the—" mumbles TB3, going on his hands and knees so that his eyes can't believe what they see a little closer. The substance is alien. But not to Reva. Very recently she took a shower in the stuff—when it was blue and spraying out of Tal5's amputated arm.

TB3's trademark hawk nose lowers deeper into the hole, sniffing for a smell that isn't there. And then, with his butt pointing up at the sky, the substance takes hold of him. As if possessed out of the blue—or in this case, out of the purple—TB3's head pops up with his sights set on an imperative task. He crawls across the grass to where the 6in action figures lay in the jacket, then slides his fingers over them with his eyes closed, the way a blind person studies another's visage. Re-Lo, Si Q, Ursa Double-Major, Julioception, Talent Master … Time Cap—TB3's careful feel settles on the villain who plays time like a fiddle.

With increased urgency, he scrambles on his hands and knees to the unearthed substance, dragging Time Cap through the excavated rocks and dirt. Reva doesn't have to, but holds her breath nevertheless.

TB3 kneels at the edge of the hole, not ten feet from the golden statue, raising the prototype action figure above his head, as if asking for his memorialized father to bless it. He then allows Time Cap to slip between his fingers and drop into the well of purple stuff.

The substance performs the process of molding to the action figure, echoing its integration with Reva's Re-Lo. With no warning, the toy bursts up and out of the hole riding a geyser. TB3 reaches from his knees and plucks Time Cap from the tall column of steam.

As TB3 clenches his fingers around the figure, a visible mesh maps the contours of his fist. In the brightness of the uprooted lamp, the pattern is notably red, contrasting the blue lines that Reva's skin had absorbed. Purple must be the color of the substance in its pure form. Tal5 had hypothesized a color code, supposing that blue meant good and red meant bad. Time Cap is a villain, so perhaps Tal5 was onto something. It's elementary: red and blue makes purple.

TB3 jumps to his feet like a man who just received a

shot of adrenaline. He badly wants the 6in Time Cap to fit inside the pocket of his rigid jeans, but the capsule-shaped helmet is simply too bulky. This obsession appears to award him with a brilliant idea. Reva doesn't need the power to read minds—TB3's envisioning figures at half the size, collectibles that can be clipped on your pocket. Dollar signs put TB3'$ eyes out—until the surrounding air molecules all at once form the individual pixels of a 360° video screen.

Lifelike images pop on every side of the encircling screen, sending TB3 into a spin. The colors and sounds light up the darkness and liven the quiet of night. Reva floats by his side in the eye of the spectacle, no stranger to the pictures on the inexplicable air display.

Flying across the sky are the real-life versions of *Arm*son, Hoodwinker, Bombastic, and Misbeehive that TB3 is certain can be touched. To every human alive Reva's age and up, the video outside of TB3's tiptoed reach is a rerun. And a disturbing one at that. Unbeknownst to TB3, this is actual footage from the Fiendish Four's acts of terror against the United States. Which happens thirty-six years from the time of this scene.

TB3 mumbles a bunch of guesses at this magical projection, each farther off target. At one point he wonders if this is a Hollywood studio's elaborate pitch to make a movie with his characters. What an achievement that would be; special effects in 1976 can't blow up a music pavilion that good (as Bombastic does now for TB3's viewing pleasure). It would crush TB3 to hear that Clash Entertainment banned further usage of *Arm*son, Hoodwinker, Bombastic, and Misbeehive following the events on display.

What happens next, at first makes Reva think that

the air is reflective, as TB3 blinks up at his own face staring back. But as the TB3 on the backdrop of stars pulls a mask evoking an American flag down over his face, Reva understands: TB3 is seeing what he will become. He's seeing HOAP.

The vision shows HOAP in his element, a control center, surrounded by gray industrial walls. There's a circular table with robotic arms and laptops, and a ring of huge video monitors overhead. A curved wall houses an array of Pocket Protectors, each secured behind glass in red-lit units (which flies completely in the face of Tal5's color-coding system). To access the action figures, HOAP has to hold his fingerprint, then his retina to biometric scanners. Reva fidgets in Re-Lo's invisible force some more while watching HOAP clip a Re-Lo cast from the same mold to his signature utility belt.

From his sprawling front lawn, decades in advance of these activities, TB3 can practically feel Re-Lo's energy via the Pocket Protector. Remarkable how the obtruding capsule-shaped helmet that won't fit in TB3's pocket is the germ of what becomes his portable power source.

Meanwhile, the scene on the screen of stars isn't done shedding light. HOAP blinks from headquarters to the Empire State Building's top deck, where Hoodwinker has dozens of fair citizens scaling the guardrails on his silent command. The blindfolded baddie hovers high above the observation deck and the faint screams from the streets, amid the throbbing *wuppa wuppa wuppa* of the news helicopter. Dramatically, HOAP gestures up at Hoodwinker, shaping his hand into a claw.

Spectating, TB3 is as stiff as the shovel that's still

stuck in the substance-saturated soil. He lets out a gasp as HOAP seizes the fiend's metaphysical energy and teleports it to a cell with four walls of two-way glass.

TB3 collapses in the grass as HOAP people-shifts the remaining three villains to their custom cells. The fanfare comes next. The accolades. The appearances. The hashtags—these really throw TB3 off balance in 1976. #Noob.

As the sky-theater turns back to night air, Reva thinks she's got things worked out. TB3 dropped Time Cap in the substance. Time Cap is in TB3's pocket. TB3 is Time Cap like she is Re-Lo. And Time Cap is conjuring images of a possible future. A future from which Reva hails. So, *actual* future is more accurate in the present.

In 2012, thirty-six years after this scene, TB3 will turn four Clash fans into supervillains by slipping them Pocket Protectors cast from the purple stuff. The Fiendish Four will cause terror. Put lives in jeopardy. And when all hope appears lost, TB3 will appear as HOAP—the Hero of All People.

For as long as Time Cap is on his pocket, TB3 will not age. Which means he has time. Time to plan. Time to build. Time to design. Time to wait. Social media in the 2010s will give his heroics more exposure than any prior decade could.

Reva can sense this time-shift ending—and a need to review what was gained by being here. This was the day when Tal finally shared his feelings. Or when TB3 finally listened. TB3 was willing to make changes. Sacrifice his fame. He tried to do the right thing. But this substance … the red version … it blinded him. Made him lose sight of how a hero would look to his troubled son. The substance swayed him to believe that the *All* in Hero of All People would include Tal.

It dawns on her now, why Re-Lo's powers picked this scene. The intention wasn't to provide her with a backstory for the present day, or to show her a future that's already in her past. Re-Lo's powers picked this scene to show her that TB3 is a parent corrupted by the substance, and that there is a product of his upbringing—Tal. TB3 is an evil creator. And there is only a single solitary worse thing she can imagine: a monster of TB3's creation. Reva was shifted here because Tal is the bigger threat! And because— possibly—Tal can be saved … if she can come to fully understand him.

And with that notion, Reva's see-through self tightens in an instant—every atom forming as one. Then, less than a half-blink later, she's off to the next scene in time.

13
VIRTUAL REALITY EXPOSURE

Under the golden statue, Reva saw the limitations of Time Cap's clairvoyance. TB3 was shown an outcome of a possible future. Nothing more. Full knowledge of exactly how TB3 sees it through was not included. So in terms of *when* Reva is currently, and *why* she is *when* she is, it's back to square one.

For starters, Reva is floating in a living room. Homey, if a little dated. She has never seen this much carpet. From what she gathers, our whole history is covered in the stuff. It does make her yearn to gather the fabric under her toes. As for the furniture, were the lavender clamshell chairs and patterned couch stolen from a dentist's office? Glass tables with gold legs— straight up gaudy. And that floral wallpaper—it has got to go. The fireplace mantle, on the other hand, looks like a perfect spot for a time traveler to get her bearings; it's lined with pictures of Tal in golden ornate frames, baby's first steps through college graduation. Also notable: TB3 is not pictured.

A woman (early forties) faces a square, convex video screen set inside a woodgrain box with two giant turn knobs on the side panel.

"Mom, do we have any Smurf-Berry Crunch?"

The man (early twenties) who enters from the

kitchen with a growling belly and empty cereal bowl is Tal, no doubt. Reva recognizes him even though he's doing something different with his hair. His new 1980s-style mullet brings to mind her dad's surviving VHS recordings of *MacGyver*. Tal is wearing three layers of polo shirts with popped collars tucked into pleated pants. Perhaps more importantly, Reva's mission should be to prevent this outfit from coming back in style.

When Tal joins his mom in front of the wood box, a casual observer—or a really anxious one in Reva's case—would assume that Tal and his mom were being subjected to something super scary. Reva glides between them for a better view, her body half through Tal and half through his mom. The box is actually an old TV. Pictured on it, beneath the noisy grain and static fuzz, is TB3. Judging by the two jaws on the floor, TB3's TV appearance is a *surprise* appearance. Out of the shot, but definitely on his person, is a Time Cap Pocket Protector, because TB3 hasn't aged a bit since Reva last saw him in 1976.

TB3 is accepting an Inkpot Award for writing and illustration at the 1986 San Diego Comic-Con. At one point, he mentions Tal and the name Nettie; this must be Tal's mom. His speech is making news because the world-famous TB3 hasn't been seen, or heard from, for eight years. As the news lady reports and the headline states, TB3 hasn't stopped publishing scripts and illustrations for Clash Comics, despite being out of the public eye since 1978.

Reva whisks across the living room and through the padlocked front door. Outside, she finds a modest yard in front of a bungalow-style home. There is no groomed shrubbery, perfectly edged flowerbeds, or golden statue of Tal Boatwright Jr.

Before she can return to the boob tube, Tal is storming out of the house with Nettie in hot pursuit.

"Where are you going?" A mother knows when a child is headed down the wrong path. *Backward*, guesses Reva, reading Nettie's troubled mind, *she's scared that Tal is going to the place from which I just came—his past.*

"Downstate," Tal retorts, spinning around.

"We sold it ages ago."

"Then why does Grandpa's statue still stand?" It's written in the worry lines on Nettie's face. Her open mouth says it all. Psychological scars were suffered in that mansion. And both mother and son had vowed never to visit it again.

Minutes earlier, a bowl of Smurf-Berry Crunch cereal would have made Tal's day. Then his dad went and muddled his life after being gone from it for eight years. No one can relate to such an upending change better than Reva. "Tell me about it," she mutters into the void.

"He was gone!" screams Tal. "Why come back? … Why now? After all this time? I need to know, Ma. I need to know why he did what he did—why he left. Why he's back now—saying our names on TV!"

"Tal!" cries Nettie as her son runs to the 1979 Chrysler LeBaron parked in the driveway (and straight through Reva getting there).

"What are you expecting to find?" The quivering in Nettie's voice begs Tal to slow his roll.

"Him!" Tal shouts from behind the wheel. "I expect to find Dad."

Tal gases it out of the drive, leaving poor Nettie in his dust. A location-shift to the passenger seat crosses Reva's mind. Calling shotgun would be funny, though her humor would be wasted in this disconnected plane she's on. Reva's powers beat her to the punchline anyway, and save her a car ride.

Reva tingles from another full-body static shock after ending up precisely where she thought she would—Tal's front passenger seat (she did call shotgun after all). It's a weird, seated hover position her body is in; she doesn't quite make contact with the upholstery.

No telling how long Tal's been parked in the shadows, staking out his old home. The sun has been swapped for the moon and the mansion is lit up bright. Tal's attention is laser-focused on the front door, past the acres of meticulous landscaping and gigantic golden statue.

If TB3's been laying low for eight years, he's not anymore. Sneaking out the back wasn't an option TB3 considered, judging by his swagger. There's no hiding in the spotlights that project TB3's hawk nose to the size of a window on the brick exterior. And the '86 Porsche 911 that emerges from the darkness—with a turbocharged roar—doesn't exactly blend in.

First, Tal waits until the black Porsche turns out of the block-paved driveway onto the road, and then he gives the key to his Chrysler a turn. They own the roads at this vague, early hour. In his tail of TB3, Tal must be mindful of distance to stay off his dad's radar.

Reva will never be safer inside a moving vehicle (and LeBarons like Tal's predate passenger-side airbags). She's along for the ride, but she's not *in* the ride. "Wearing a seatbelt is dumb," would be a false statement, save for this singularly unique scenario. The seatbelt would just cross into her invisible body if she could actually put it on. Tal could collide with a tree and she would walk—or float—away unscathed.

You could say that Reva is out of harm's way, but she would disagree. Her fight in this battle is mental, not physical. Just like it always is for Reva, who on a daily basis has to overcome an unrelenting, general nervousness. Nervousness, not about one thought in particular, nervousness about everything.

This scene from Tal's car, on this eerily dark road, makes Reva more anxious than any first day of school, teeth cleaning, or dinner out at a restaurant (she's always had a thing about restaurants). Changing the past isn't a tool in Re-Lo's toolkit. Observe, investigate; that's her arsenal. Reva simply has to be her smart self. Get in, get the clues, and get out—Re-Lo's forte.

At the source of Reva's anxiety is fear. A fear that something bad will happen if she doesn't repeat a certain action; for example, tapping her toes on the floor. If asked this second, she would describe a time-shift as virtual reality exposure to the very essence of that fear. Her surroundings at the moment suggest bad things afoot—and she's in the thick of it. So while she isn't necessarily squaring off against a foe with superhuman strength, these trials of her stress resilience are, for her, infinitely more challenging.

TB3 in his Porsche and Tal in his LeBaron are riding a two-lane country road bordered by rock walls and trees. The only light is from the moon and the car's headlamps. Keeping a keen eye, Reva notices signs indicating that they're in Stony Point, New York, about forty miles outside of New York City.

Next, TB3's taillights blink off, cloaking the road ahead of Tal in blackness. Tal pulls the car onto a grassy shoulder in the area of TB3's disappearing act, where a rock wall ends. Visibility is low and doesn't reach beyond the dust hanging in the hazy headlamps. Reva has the advantage of phasing through the upholstered roof to see outside, but there's nothing worth noting except trees barely streaked with moonlight.

The sound of a door unlatching snaps the silence. Tal is outside the car, keeping contact with the long hood, short of breath in the night air. Any second now, Reva's expecting that horror will befall Tal. For what other reason would she be shadowing Tal's direction through life? A pitch-black country road isn't going to be the scene of a warm father-and-son embrace. Reva would bet her whole comic collection that Tal is the real monster lying in wait where—or *when*—she's from. In her analogy, HOAP is the Dr. Frankenstein of this backstory. Add it all together and no wonder she's got scary movies on the brain.

If Reva's right, the road ahead is gloomy—like the gloomy road ahead of Tal's car. So when the gloom comes from behind in a burst of electric blue, one could say that the gloom comes from out of the blue. A black-hooded TB3 catches Tal's lifeless body and then drags it toward the rear of the Chrysler. It was a stun weapon that knocked Tal unconscious—same weapon that arms HOAP's henchmen in the present.

Tal is lugged across the road to a dirt path where TB3's Porsche idles with an open passenger door. Clumsily, TB3 props Tal in the bucket seat. *How did TB3 get away with this? Wasn't it obvious what happened to Tal? The police couldn't figure this one out? Seriously?* As soon as the questions occur to Reva, so does the answer: the purple stuff. With this substance, TB3 is above the law. Reva concludes that she might be the only person alive who truly knows what happened on this night in 1986.

And on that note, TB3 slams the car door shut, in sync with the end of this time-shift.

A blink takes Reva from the forest road to a forest of giant skyscrapers. From a dark night to a night lit with dazzling colors. New York City, The Big Apple; she recognizes it from movies and TV. In her observation, it's impossible to miss the massive neon logos for Clash Comics and TB3 Toys shining brightly above. The logos are throwback designs from the 1980s, validating her intuition that the date hasn't changed.

Reva has always wanted to visit the Clash Comics headquarters, in her regular body that is. Nonetheless, it's cool to see it in person, or in ghost-person. If there were time to spare, she would phase inside for a self-guided tour. But right on cue, TB3's Porsche roars down W 51st St and brakes at her location.

TB3—in the same black hoodie—exits the sports car, causing cabbies to lean angrily on their steering wheels. Tal remains passed out in the passenger seat; the concert of cab horns doesn't even wake him. Stopped traffic at his back, TB3 stretches skyward as if attempting to catch the full moon. Then, with a dramatic gesture, he casts a limitless bubble that freezes all time. Pedestrians stop walking. Lights stop blinking. Cab horns stop honking. Reva doesn't need visual confirmation—there's a Time Cap on his pants pocket under the hem of that hoodie. For sure.

In the 1978 Re-Lo annual comic, TB3 wrote a story that gave Time Cap a new time-freeze power. Using lunar gravitational influence when the moon was full, Time Cap could bring the entire planet to a standstill. But there were rules. Time couldn't be resumed if the result of any action taken during a time-freeze would derail a living thing from its timeline. In such instances, moved items had to be returned, used materials had to be replenished, and so forth. A special vision mode would indicate the measures required of Time Cap to set time ticking again.

TB3 strolls back to his car in peace and quiet, with a time-freeze enveloping the rest of Manhattan and presumably the world. Flicking a dashboard switch, the chunk of road under his tires abruptly loosens and begins lowering into the earth. As father and son sink below the street inside the Porsche, a matching section of pavement slides over the opening, covering their tracks.

Reva phases through W 51st St, where she discovers a subterranean car lift that must be two thousand miles tall. Downward she moves with the Porsche until it reaches the bottom, where she can faintly make out the New York City cabbies already honking at a new inconvenience.

14
THE FIRST PRISONER

Heavy sliding doors split open, revealing the control center Reva saw in Time Cap's vision. Well, the bones of it anyway. TB3's Porsche drives off the lift and into the spacious underground construction site. The smooth, industrial floor glistens under the fluorescent lighting installed high up in the exposed rafters. There are rows of metal scaffoldings, extended scissor lifts, and forklifts parked around the area. Beyond the hub, Reva notes a framework for expansion, excavated tunnels and the basic structures of future rooms. On dimensions alone, Reva can make a pretty good guess where she and her dad are presently held prisoner.

A tangle of cords runs every which way, connecting banks of computers from the 1980s to unprotected electrical outlets. From Reva's standpoint, or floatpoint, the only finished part down here is the array of Pocket Protectors. Each action figure is secured behind glass in red-lit wall units along a sleek, curved wall. TB3's collection consists of the five Protectors and four villains: *Arr*son, Hoodwinker, Bombastic, and Misbeehive. The villains look adorable as thumb-size toys—especially Misbeehive's cute little antennae and fuzzy yellow-and-black suit. As harmless as they appear, it's easy to see evil in these specific Pocket Protectors, having foreknowledge of their future use. Spare wall units indicate that TB3 plans on adding to his collection. Up close, the convex glass shields come across as bulletproof.

A wall calendar confirms this is July of 1986, and there's a circle drawn around the square marking the full moon. Bolsters Reva's theory that TB3 exploited Time Cap's time-freeze to get below Manhattan unseen.

TB3 opens the passenger door and Tal practically falls out of the vehicle. Tal is woozy from having only just regained consciousness, best expressed by his three layers of popped collars that are all smushed down.

"What do you think?" says TB3, one hand guiding Tal into the control room, the other showing it off as if he were revealing a prize on a game show. "Everything you see was DIY."

Their steps over to the array of Pocket Protectors create echoes in the vast empty space. "I froze time in 1978 so I could build it," says TB3, plucking a Time Cap off his back pocket.

"Aha!" exclaims Reva. "Called it." The action figure with the capsule-shaped helmet, little suit nodes, and mini energy wrist-rings means that TB3 wrote the time-freeze power into Time Cap's character for his own usage. Sort of remixes an old adage: The pen that is mightier than the sword makes the sword even mightier. Explains why TB3 didn't use Re-Lo to kidnap Tal; TB3 can't teleport people until Re-Lo can in the 1990s comics. As Reva can attest from experience, TB3 will have the idea for people-shifting eventually.

"The toys give me powers," states TB3, towing Tal to the unit that holds Talent Master, the one with the transparent face and shiny hooded cloak. "He boosts the talents of the people above. Architecture.

Construction. Plumbing. Electrical. Engineering. Computer science. Security. ..."

Tal slaps himself repeatedly. He probably thinks that he passed out when TB3 appeared on TV, he didn't actually wake where he did, and he's stuck in the craziest dream. Reva knows the feeling; she had her own rude awakening in HOAP's headquarters earlier. (Though with all this time-shifting, it definitely does NOT feel like the same day!)

"No one else knows of this place. That makes you special, son. Forgive me for how I went about bringing you here. Please understand that I had to keep its location a secret."

Reva zips behind Tal, sensing that he's about to topple over backward from shock. As Reva holds out her weightless arms to catch him, she remembers that if Tal did fall, it would be right through her. TB3 slings Tal to a seat at a circular table outfitted with robotic arms. Compared to the modern robots James left behind in Reva's garage, these models are thick and clunky.

"I'm sorry I've been gone," says TB3, pulling up a chair. "I wanted headquarters to at least be up and running before reconnecting. I could have kept time frozen after the site prep. Kept our time on hold. But I had to let it slip on. I can't delay the year 2013 any longer. The year I become HOAP—the Hero of All People. When everyone has these little computers that they use to paint themselves picture-perfect lives on a global computer network. I will save all of these people from supervillains! And all of these people will share every heroic move I make!"

Tal's quivering lips can only form a series of *waa* sounds that want to be the first in a million questions.

What the heck kind of a name is HOAP? That's the question Reva would ask if she were in Tal's position. As her mind happens on the topic of Tal's position, Tal goes from slumped in a seat to collapsed on the floor.

TB3 braces Tal like a crutch, shuffling his lame son to the wall adjoining the Pocket Protector array. "I can't just sit here twiddling my thumbs for thirty-something years. We can build a medical bay. A workshop. A training arena. Cells strong enough for supervillains. A lounge. But most importantly, you and I can build a life here."

By pushing on a gray panel that blends with the industrial tile, TB3 makes an entire wall slide into the floor. Exposed to view is a sizable bedroom within a glass cube—a glorified, furnished version of the cell from which Reva's physical body is time-shifting.

"Never again will civilization see my face without the mask. The anti-aging that Time Cap affords me would give away my secret identity. Headquarters will double as our home. We will gather food and supplies when the moon is full. And when necessary, make purchases in *disguise*. ..."

The last time TB3 stroked his chin was in Tal's bedroom, when the concept for a character named Revisionist organically came to him. TB3's hand is at his chin again, suggesting that a master of disguise could be inspiriting his imagination. He puts a pin in it, though, with more to tell Tal.

"... I could have granted Time Cap unlimited use of his time-freeze power. No rules. No restrictions. But I sought discipline. Routine. And I didn't give the idea for a time-skip ability a second thought. Why would I sabotage our opportunity to make up for lost time?"

Reva phases through the glass to scope out this

revealed bedroom from the inside. There's a separate bath with shower, a comfortable-looking bed, and a drafting table for drawing. The flooring is wide plank wood, covered partly by a cool rug with the Protectors' iconic symbols in a colorful grid pattern.

A bookshelf in the corner might be the same piece she commingled with in '76. It collects the same Clash comics, minus the mustaches that young Tal scribbled on the characters.

"This is all yours," TB3 says to Tal, dragging him another step closer toward the glass. "Safe from that horrible, dog-eat-dog world. … We can make comics here. You and me. A dream team. We'll be legendary."

Done with being Tal's support, TB3 steps to the side, letting his son stumble forward. Tal's palms meet the clear wall; his eyes open wide. This room—the slanted ceiling above the bed—it's an updated reproduction of his childhood bedroom. Words still can't find their way out of Tal's throat.

This happens to Reva often. When the teacher asks her to summarize a chapter out loud, for example. On paper, wonderful interpretations flow freely from her pencil, and in great detail. As speech, the same effortless grasp of a subject locks up like a Time Cap time-freeze. In these situations, she allows the fear of making mistakes to take control.

Once this puzzle is put together, Reva will have seconds at most to download her friends over SpaceTime. She'll have a plan, and it will be clever and calculated; the ability to communicate the plan is what worries her. Stella, oppositely, could put this whole case in song and sing it to a sold-out stadium. Reva can't play the recorder in front of her stuffed animals.

Tal has real reason to be speechless in this scene. It's

not astonishment or amazement. It's because speaking is nearly impossible when your inner dialogue says, *Ohmigod. This is not a dream. I'm a prisoner in my crazy dad's secret hideout.*

"I'm glad you like it," says TB3, either misreading the terror that Tal is wearing on his sleeve, or choosing to ignore it. Then, seizing an opportunity, TB3 taps a pattern on the keypad outside the bedroom. With Tal's full weight against it, the unlocked door swings open and sends Tal somersaulting inside.

Taking a swift grip of the almost unnoticeable handle, TB3 pulls the door shut and doesn't let go until a loud beep assures him that it's locked.

"No!" screams Tal, jumping to his feet and slapping the thick glass over and over. "No! No! No! Nooo!"

15
THERAPY

Reva doesn't move an inch from Tal's bedroom in HOAP's headquarters—she moves twenty-six years. She can calculate the time that's passed by the 2012 calendar on the industrial wall. A blink ago, the same screw held up a 1986 calendar. It must be July 21, 2012, because the previous squares are slashed. On this date in history, Reva turned four. And her dad vanished from their kitchen.

Tal sits at the end of his bed with his feet on the floor. Half a life spent underground in this glass room hasn't been kind to him looks-wise. He's forty-nine years old, but most people would guess fifty-nine. Long gone are the spiky shag from the 70s and the feathered mullet from the 80s; his hair is gray now and receded.

As Reva spins to get eyes on TB3, he walks right through her. On the other extreme, Tal's ageless father has benefitted from the Time Cap Pocket Protector; he looks like a youthful thirty-six when he's actually ... seventy-two (Reva's fingers were needed for the math). The fit of TB3's civilian clothes gives the impression that he's in prime "HOAP shape." *There's gotta be a gym somewhere down here too*, Reva figures.

Headquarters has undergone some serious updates. Scaffoldings and lifts are put away. Computer banks are upgraded with state-of-the-art systems. Robotic arms have moved from the Stone Age to the Space Age. Overhead, a 360° ring of large video screens has been installed and the once-exposed ceiling is finished with mesh paneling. The excavated tunnels and basic structures of 1986 are now well-lit passageways to functional rooms. From Reva's vantage she can make out a workshop where there are long tables with mounted screens and piles of parts. Around the corner is a lounge with a sectional couch and full bar. Signage also points to a gym, medical bay, training arena, and cellblock. And all signs point to TB3 being fully operational.

"I must leave for LA to make final preparations," TB3 says to Tal, pulling on a black hood.

Curious what powers TB3's packing for the West Coast, Reva takes a quick inventory of the Pocket Protector array along the curved wall. The five Protectors and four villains (*Arrr*son, Hoodwinker, Bombastic, Misbeehive) are present behind glass, plus two action figures that weren't in units twenty-six years ago.

One of them is Mimic Man, a plain man in a gray suit, white dress shirt, red tie, and wool flat cap. Mimic Man was a central villain of Julioception comics in the 1990s and 2000s. He could take the exact likeness— height, weight, and voice—of any living person.

Reva's favorite Mimic Man storyline? Easy— *Disguised to Hypnotize*. Julioception had figured out a way to sense Mimic Man in disguise, so Mimic Man countered by stealing the likeness of a world-famous hypnotist. Exploiting the hypnotist's face, voice, renowned reputation, and full slate of packed venues,

Mimic Man captured impressionable minds across the country. By broadcasting a trigger word over TV and radio, Mimic Man had an instant army to do his bidding on demand.

The real hypnotist—hidden where no one would ever find him—trained his heart to beat in Morse code, knowing that Julioception's enhanced senses would eventually pinpoint it. The coded message was: Hand of Sand. Applying his great sense for both secret messages and the fine arts, Julioception headed to where there stands a sculpture of a hand breaking from the sand— the Chilean desert.

Julioception traced the hypnotist's heartbeat to a sealed desert cave. The dramatic quest brought a national audience to the edges of their collective seats. Through their sets, the rescued hypnotist spoke to those under Mimic Man's control, and freed all from the trance.

Reva, in front of the last wall unit being used, tries to scratch her see-through head. She can't figure out what character the other new Pocket Protector is supposed to be. And she's been reading Clash comics her whole life. Black suit, bushy hair, binocular eyes connected to a power source on his neck. Not ringing any bells. The red circle on his chest could be a target or the letter *O*.

TB3 puts his finger, then retina to the biometric scanners at the left of the units. The glass shields slide open as TB3 starts down the line, pocketing Re-Lo, Si Q, Julioception, and Mimic Man.

"Don't get into any trouble while I'm gone," snickers TB3, repeating the biometric scans to secure the action figures that are staying behind.

"Twenty-six years," snaps Tal, standing from his bed. "Twenty-six years I've been the good son. Doing everything asked of me. Building all of this. Yet you keep me locked in my room like I'm still your little boy!"

Tal slaps his hands against the glass in the same manner he did twenty-six years ago (or a couple of minutes ago on Reva's clock).

"Patience, son," says TB3. "The hero never starts with a sidekick. I've told you, HOAP works alone in the beginning. You come along in the sequel."

"At what? Sixty? What will you call me? Greatest American Geezer? Captain Curmudgeon? Old Fart Man?"

"I've told you a thousand times to wear Time Cap!" spits the youthful TB3, meeting Tal's droopy and wrinkled face at the glass. The little red lightning bolts darting through TB3's neck veins are a good reason not to mess with villain Pocket Protectors. "If not for Time Cap, I'd be watching golf. Grumbling about my aching joints. Instead, I'm on the cusp of reigning supreme."

"I've cherished life down here," breathes Tal, simmering down some. "I wouldn't want things any other way." Either Tal is being quite sincere, or he's an incredible actor. "My rule about your Pocket Protectors stands. I won't touch them."

"Pocket *Protectooor*, you mean," corrects TB3, throwing a suspicious glare through the divider. "My Pocket Protector*sss*—*plural*—are off limits. I offered you the use of one and one only. Be a geriatric sidekick for all I care. But don't come crawling back when your walker isn't cutting it as a superhero vehicle."

TB3 presses his butt to the bedroom wall, flaunting the Time Cap that's clipped on the back pocket of his jeans. "Thirty-five years and counting. Not a single side effect. The red lightning just means it's working. When you're ready to stop being such a wuss about it, I'll cast one for you. But I wouldn't wait too much longer. ... You've got some serious crow's feet goin' on there."

Re-Lo and Si Q get attached to TB3's left front pocket, then Julioception goes on the other. As Mimic Man slides into place next to Julioception, TB3 gets an idea.

"I'm not going to need any disguises this trip," says TB3, pulling Mimic Man off his pocket. "And it's high time you conquer this fear of powers."

In the cell door is a low slot about the width of a dinner tray; TB3 flips Mimic Man through it onto Tal's hardwood floor, where the action figure lands plain-face up.

"Try it on for size if you get the nerve," sneers TB3. "Who says you gotta be Captain Curmudgeon? You always wanted to be a movie star. Mimic Man can make you look like one. Don't worry. Julioception is with me. Just call if puttin' the wittle toy on your pocket makes you scared. I'll hear my wittle guy and come wunnin'."

"I know the drill," sighs Tal, resigning to a stack of comics at the end of his bed. Reva recognizes the comic Tal escapes into; it's #9 of a twelve-part Ursa Double-Major event from that summer. It was in James's last comic book pull list before his vanishing. The cover with Sagittarius—the half-human half-horse—is stamped on her memory.

An explosive rush swings Reva's attention from the shiny centaur to the control room. TB3's gone from it. Said he had to go to LA for final preparations. Must have blinked there with his Re-Lo.

Tal is reading. TB3 is on the opposite coast. Reva is

starting to panic. Why hasn't she blinked out of this scene? Was an important clue missed? What did she learn here? It helps to review. For starters, she can ID middle-aged Tal; but that does her no good if Tal ever decides to pick up that Mimic Man off his floor. Playing the scene back in her head, nothing else jumps out except for that new Pocket Protector with the binocular eyes.

Going in for a closer inspection of the action figure with the *O* on its chest, Reva hears another explosive rush over her shoulder. *That was fast.* She spins, expecting TB3 back at the big round table with the robotic arms.

When bad things happen, it's a natural reaction to want a reason. Through a handful of time-shifts, Reva's been after an explanation for why she's doing this and not celebrating her birthday at Comic-Con. By the end of her pirouette, she's staring at the answer. This—the string of time-shifts—is therapy.

James is standing barefooted in HOAP's control room at arm's reach, with an expression of complete and utter shock on his face. ... And a Re-Lo Pocket Protector with a smeared left eye clipped on the pocket of his pajama pants.

16
THE TERMINATOR

Tal slides off the end of his bed to the Protector symbols on the colorful rug. Aghast. No one from the outside has ever stepped foot, with or without shoes, in headquarters—so says the silent shock from his open mouth.

Legs going rubbery, Tal pulls himself across the floor to where his space ends. "W-who are you?"

Takes James a minute to respond. Wondering which C3U movie set he's standing on. "... Where am I?"

Halfway through his climb up the squeaky glass, Tal spots the Re-Lo on James's PJs. "One must have gotten out. ..." he mumbles.

"Tell me where I am!" demands James.

"Shhh! Shhh!" begs Tal with a stiff finger to his lips. "We mustn't let him hear us."

"What? ... Who? ..." James's attention darts left and right, assuming there's a sleeping baby or a stern librarian in the vicinity.

"What did you think of when you put the Re-Lo on your pocket?" whispers Tal, oozing curiosity.

James doesn't have time for games. He hates exposition in his comics, but he could sure go for some over-explaining at the moment.

Tal pleads for James to keep a lid on another

outburst by performing a series of frantic gestures. "You thought it would be cool to save the world, didn't you?" he breathes.

"Yes. And how did you know?" James didn't say that aloud, his astonishment alone did. Adding, with more stunned silence, "Okay. I'm listening."

"Re-Lo's power brought you here," Tal explains.

There's barely enough mobility in James's stiffened neck to consider the Re-Lo with the smeared left eye on his cotton pocket.

"Re-Lo was the first Pocket Protector my father cast from the substance. Took a bunch of tries to get it right. … I thought he destroyed all the duds. That's what he said. … But one must have slipped through the cracks. …"

"The Pocket Protectors Palace Playset—it was in the attic. I literally just brought it down—"

"Shhh!" Tal's finger trembles against his lips. "My father has a Julioception with him. If he hears, you'll never leave this place alive."

"I was in my kitchen," says James in muted tones. "A second ago. … My little girl. Reva. I left her alone. I need to get back. She's only four."

Reva glides to her dad with designs of squeezing him tight, but she only phases clean through his body. Suddenly it's obvious—in James's helplessness and confusion and panic—what Reva's powers want her to see. Bad stuff doesn't make any sense. And no matter what we do to prevent something bad from happening, more often than not, it's out of our control.

"Your Re-Lo Pocket Protector is cast with something that gives you her powers," Tal whispers.

James picks Re-Lo off his pocket and brings it higher; the color-changing bands that spiral down and around each arm to arrowheads immediately turn brown, meaning *scared* by mood-ring definition. He can't begin to imagine how an action figure could give a person superpowers, but then is reminded by his bare feet that he didn't walk here.

"Doesn't sound so crazy does it?" says Tal. "You know I'm telling the truth. Because you're a man who knows a location-shift when he sees one. ... Or *does* one—"

"I wore this Re-Lo until middle school," says James. "Never teleported. Pretty sure I'd remember if I had."

"Please, before you blink back, let me out of here. Please." Tal plasters his desperation against the wall. "My name is Tal Boatwright. If you know Re-Lo, you know my father. TB3. Clash Comics. Pocket Protectors. Toy Boat Toy Boat Toy Boit Toys. He's kept me here. His prisoner. Twenty-six years. You must have heard of my disappearance on the news."

Every nerd has heard of TB3, which includes James. Clash fans believe he's the underground writer whose credit gets blacked out on covers. When James was a fifth- and sixth-grader, the big stories were the baby who fell in the well and Tal's disappearance. Police found Tal's car on the side of the road, but never him. TB3 was ruled out as a suspect almost immediately. Not until Tal implicated TB3 just now did James consider the connection. Which is strange, because it seems like a straightforward lead for detectives to pursue.

Whenever the well-baby's face wasn't on TV, Tal's was. But that was nearly three decades ago. Even if he had a photographic memory, James couldn't ID Tal. That's to say, Tal doesn't look like a recent college graduate anymore.

James proceeds with his own investigation.

Protectors rug. Bookshelf of Clash back issues. Framed 8x10 of TB3 and a twenty-three-year-old Tal (a selfie in front of the Pocket Protector array).

"I graduated from Juilliard in '86," Tal whispers. "Drama. Before I could land a single audition, I was performing here. Pretending to be grateful for my father's 'hospitality.' Acting my butt off to stay alive. It was either join him or ..." TB3's capacity for villainy will forever make Tal shudder. "Him letting me go would never happen. ... I knew too much. My only play was to gain his trust. Bide my time. Hope to get my hands on the Pocket Protectors someday. With Re-Lo I could blink out of here. Find out where *here* is. And rain hellfire down on it. ... Please ... I'm begging you, before you blink back, open the door!"

Tal's story is convincing, aided by the dark undertones. However, he also admitted to being a good actor. So James isn't sure what to believe.

"The code is: 1, 2, 3, 4," states Tal, turning James's focus to the keypad.

Tough call. If Tal is telling the truth about the Pocket Protectors, then it's not a good idea for anyone to have them.

"We can destroy the Pocket Protectors," adds Tal, reading James's conflicted thoughts. "But first we take down my dad. ... Or nothing else will matter. You can choose not to help me. And I wouldn't blame you. But know that your home won't be happy for long. He's turning people into supervillains. Real-life versions of *Arrr*son, Hoodwinker, Bombastic, and Misbeehive!"

Reva wishes she had a voice. She would tell her dad that all of what Tal says is true. Then she remembers that this is 2012. Even if James agrees to help Tal, the Fiendish Four still happens. HOAP still happens.

James's imprisonment still happens. And her being exposed to this traumatic stimulus still happens.

The tight spot makes James's head spin, but it hasn't twisted his knowledge of comics. "If I have Re-Lo's powers, then I can go back in time. I can fact-check your whole story."

"I'd welcome you to," Tal replies, "but there's no telling how many shifts your Re-Lo has left. Might have ten. One. Maybe none. You don't want to be here when TB3 returns. If two's company, three's a dead guy in his jammies."

How exactly did James get to this dilemma? Reva had run off to find crayons, scarlet for hair and black for a ninja catsuit. James was waxing nostalgic about classic comics, middle school, and Pocket Protectors. Thinking about how, in a blink, he had become a hero to a little girl and a little boy. With Re-Lo on his pocket, James wished that he could protect his children from anything this world would throw at them. Next thing he knew, he was at HOAP's headquarters, facing an opportunity to do just that (and feeling the worst full-body static shock in history). That's how Re-Lo's power works. And who is James to doubt Re-Lo?

Leaping to the keypad, James enters the basic four-digit code (TB3 kept it simple). The door unlocks and opens outward. Tal steps over the Mimic Man action figure and into the control room for the first time without TB3 present.

Paths to bring down TB3 are open, but each has obstacles. Unfortunately, Mimic Man can't fool biometric scanners (the character discovered that limitation in *Julioception #23: Access Denied*), so accessing the rest of TB3's Pocket Protectors by that means isn't possible.

Using James's Re-Lo, they could report TB3's location and schemes to the FBI. It should not be ignored that TB3 has Si Q, Julioception, Time Cap, and a Re-Lo of his own clipped on his front and back pockets. Without lifting a finger, TB3 could stop them from spilling a single syllable.

Consider the Re-Lo at their disposal. For thirty-two years it's been an ordinary Pocket Protector. If the action figure is truly from TB3's failed first attempts with the substance, then either it needed time to power up, or it had a temporary burst and now it's dead.

They could try teleporting TB3 to one of his custom cells. See how he adjusts to an artic freeze. But Time Cap throws a wrench in the works. In Tal's, or James's, first go with the substance, they wouldn't stand a chance against Re-Lo's archnemesis. TB3 is a Time Cap pro.

Tal and James have been quietly brainstorming along the same lines as Reva. Blink to pickpocket is another option, as viable as any. If they swiped Si Q from TB3, hacking the security system would be a cinch. With the shields down on the Pocket Protector units, they would be like kids in a superpower store. A pocket with Ursa could have TB3 seeing stars. A pocket with Talent Master could have TB3 crying uncle (assuming there are mixed martial arts talents in range to borrow). Since this is likely Tal and James's only shot at this, they can't fail.

But they will fail. Is that why Reva hasn't left this scene? *Is failure supposed to be less threatening if I watch my dad crash and burn?* These powers keep telling her that solving the Reva mystery is as important as solving the Boatwright mystery.

"We could build a robot," inserts James, twisting Tal's wrinkles into knots. "I'm a robotics engineer. ..."

James studies a few components from the pile of parts on the big round table. "We have everything we need." A few taps on the nearest monitor calls up robotic simulation software; the screen wakes to a computer-aided drawing of an automated beehive smoker system. "He's got the latest software. We can do this."

James hunts around the vast control room. "... If only we had more of this ... substance you spoke of."

"There's a whole tank of the stuff in the workshop," Tal says, voice super low on the subject of TB3's precious substance.

"Perfect," says James, matching Tal's volume. "We can use it as a catalyst. I'll make a chamber for docking a Pocket Protector. A mechanism can pump the substance into the chamber. Like blood to a heart. The robot will get the powers of whatever action figure is docked."

The Mimic Man on the floor of Tal's bedroom—James's bare feet make a beeline for it.

"Stop!" warns Tal in his loudest whisper, suspending James's hand inches from the figure with the gray suit, white dress shirt, red tie, and wool flat cap. "That's a full-strength villain Pocket Protector. Whole different ball game. Unless you never want your daughter to recognize you again, use gloves." Tal points to a locker stuffed with hardhats, protective masks, and work gloves.

"We program the robot to take your place here," James explains while pulling on a pair of gloves and tossing Tal his own. "With your likeness. By docking Mimic Man in the chamber. ... I'll write a single objective in its code: Terminate TB3. When it achieves that objective, it powers down permanently. ... Something tells me your dad's built these digs somewhere no one will ever look. So we make it his tomb. …"

"It's a little dark, don't you think?"

"How much time do we have? I could write something more complex. Program the robot to hold your dad captive. In your room there. Ration his food supply. Keep him comfortable."

"He stays a few days when he visits the target sites. Likes getting food service. Binging the latest Clash shows. I can usually predict when he's coming back by the number of frozen dinners in my fridge. Off that, I'd say we have seventy-two hours."

"*Terminate* it is then," states James. "I would need double that, at least, to write a captor-slash-caretaker program."

Tal's expression is immediately fraught with second thoughts.

"Well, is he going to attack the world with supervillains or not?" asks James. "You seemed pretty desperate a minute ago. What was all that about raining hellfire?"

Tough pill to swallow, but Tal agrees; there isn't a better plan than a Mimic Man-powered terminator robot. … Or is there? … "His molds!" Tal thinks out loud, barely more audible than a thought. "… We could cast a Julioception. Bring my dad to his senses."

"And where are the molds?"

"I dunno," admits Tal. "Gotta be here somewhere."

"We're making the robot," James decides. "So you can tell the world your story. Play yourself in the movie. Public opinion will see this for what it is. Self-defense." James pinches the Re-Lo with the smeared left eye from his pocket. "Promise me it never touches that stuff. We use whatever juice it's got left to blink outta here. After that, I don't want it bringing anyone anywhere again."

A nod from Tal says that he wants the same.

"Now," James urges, "show me to that workshop."

17
OBJECTIFIER

There's a part in the second Si Q movie when Street Angel promises not to tag a school with graffiti. A second later, the whole school is graffitied in spray paint.

In the movie business this technique is called a *smash cut*. A smash cut, cuts out all of the in-between stuff that a character lives through—cutting the viewer from one moment to another for a narrative purpose.

Sometimes smash cuts are used for a comedic effect. Sometimes smash cuts are used to skip a really boring part; for example, a robotics engineer building a robot. The audience wants to see a robot, not how it's made. Bring a book!

To Reva, this blink feels like a smash cut. Tal pointed James in the direction of HOAP's workshop to build a robot, and now she floats in said workshop, face to face with said robot. She has already made the acquaintance of James's creation that stands before her with its eyes closed. It's Tal5.

On the nearest worktable lie the Mimic Man Pocket Protector and framed selfie of Tal and TB3. It could be that the later served as a visual guide for sculpting Tal5's default image.

The workshop is a grid of long rectangular tables

lined with mounted screens and covered by laptops, scrap piles, silicon chips, motherboards, synthetic rubber and fiber, and various prosthetic limbs. A storeroom in the corner houses a cylindrical vat of the purple substance.

It's hard to focus on anything else with Tal5 sitting there. Looking all innocent—a spitting image of a thirteen-year-old Tal. Except that Tal wasn't hardcoded to kill.

Human, middle-aged Tal isn't in the room. Must be tearing the place apart for TB3's hidden stash of Pocket Protector molds. Searching for an alternative to the assassination-by-robot plan. He seemed pretty convinced that Julioception's powers could do the trick.

While Reva's mind is here, Tal5 is likely on one of these benches in the present, waiting to bleed out when time resumes. *Virtual reality therapy, bring it on!* she thinks, bracing for the latest in traumatic stimulus.

"Now to make you Mimic Man," says James, pinching the gray-suited action figure between his gloved thumb and forefinger.

James pulls up Tal5's TB3 Toys tee (headquarters is definitely lacking a walk-in closet). A segment of synthetic skin peels back from a small chamber designed for docking Pocket Protectors. When Mimic Man's clip touches the semiconductor on the inside of the unit, a heart-like pump is triggered, circulating the catalyst. Immediately, the chamber fills with the purple stuff.

Determined to get her head around James's work, Reva's ghostly head literally gets around James's work. Her close inspection of the remarkable chamber ends abruptly when James's hand goes through her face to replace the skin-cover.

Tal5's eyes pop open. "Happy birthday!" he exclaims, in a voice Reva last heard singing along to Aerosmith.

Frosty the Snowman, she smiles, catching the reference that her dad wrote in Tal5's code.

Studying his maker intently, Tal5 spots a zigzag pattern streaking James's arms. "Hmmm," Tal5 vocalizes, filing the observation under: Important. Naturally, James is true-blue—and the basis for Tal5's idea of a hero-palette.

"Assume the current likeness of Tal Boatwright IV," whispers James in the robot's ear.

Magically, Tal5's boyish face morphs into a middle-aged form of it, receding hairline, crow's feet, and all. His belly swells to replicate two-plus decades of frozen meals. And his sweatpants rip at the cuffs as the prostheses extend to reach Tal's current height.

My dad's a genius, Reva thinks. It's almost impossible to believe that this was happening while her four-year-old self was undergoing the emotional shock of his vanishing. Such a mind-blowing point of view. Two different Re-Lo Pocket Protectors—one hurting Reva and one helping Reva, eight years apart. The Re-Lo on the worktable is to blame for traumatizing toddler Reva. The Re-Lo on Reva's shorts wants tween Reva to realize that even dads who can make shape-shifting robots can't always control the course life takes.

"Always think outside the box," says James, winking directly at Reva. He must sense her by virtue of the dual Re-Los, working in tandem to unbalance evil. How else could he possibly be wise to her presence?

James wasn't around during Reva's upbringing, but his lessons were stored in these scenes for her to eventually absorb. He's training her to think outside the box. Because it's the only chance she's got at defeating HOAP. In the event that he fails to do so.

Cue Tal, who enters the workshop not expecting an animated robot that could pass as his clone. Caught by surprise, Tal lets out a scream—a high-pitched, drawn-out scream. Tal5, following Tal's cue, imitates the high-pitched, drawn-out scream. Reva's thoughts go straight to the screening of *E.T.* at her drive-in birthday party last year, the part when Gertie first encounters E.T.

Birthday parties and movies sound nice, but she's beginning to embrace her position of power.

"I heard the screams," sneers TB3. An explosive rush brought him back, in the same outfit he was wearing a couple of days ago when he blinked to LA—pocket accessories included. "Everything okay?"

"I can explain—" frets Tal.

"No need," says TB3, straightening his Re-Lo. "I'll see for myself." Like lag in one of Sam's online matches, TB3 drops for a frame and then reappears.

"My own son," scorns TB3, stepping to Tal's robot twin, "plotting to terminate me—tsk, tsk."

Tal was really scared the night he was brought here twenty-six years ago. Reva would estimate that, in this moment, Tal is twenty-six times that level of scared.

"I gave you what you always wanted," TB3 goes on, yanking up Tal5's tee. "I gave you love!" Forming a fist, he punches ("Unngh!") through the rubber chest. "I gave you attention!" With the docked Mimic Man pinched, TB3 plucks the action figure from Tal5's chamber. "And this is how you repay me?"

Tal5 transforms to his default settings. TB3 recognizes the teenage boy who used to create comics in his room all day (minus the spiky shag 'do). "I would be remiss for not complimenting your work, Mr.

Robot," TB3 says to James.

"I wanted you to see me," says Tal. "At the end. In your final breaths. The innocent boy whose life you ruined."

"I've always wanted a grandson," TB3 snickers with a caress of Tal5's synthetic cheekbone. "I think I'll keep him. As it happens, a sidekick position just opened. … Tal Boatwright V. No … Tal5. That's how they name all the newfangled gadgets these days."

With ears reddened, TB3 clears James and Tal5 from the workshop in a rush fueled by anger. Blinked into their cells, Reva presumes. TB3's black hoodie is shed to the floor—exposing the binocular-eyed Pocket Protector that he has clipped on the pocket space alongside Julioception.

"His name is Objectifier," states TB3, spelling out the meaning behind the red O across the character's chest. "Intended to be your villain. For the sequel. In 2020." Reva had pictured the overhyped reveal of the new Clash villain going very differently. To begin with, she thought she'd be at Comic-Con, not in TB3's past.

"2020? That's eight years from now! Don't make me wait that long." Tal's disappointment is very theatrical. "Please, father, introduce me sooner. All I want is to be by your side."

"Save it!" snaps TB3. "The act won't work on me anymore. 2013 is my year. And my year alone! As Time Cap foretold."

"Then the year after," pleads Tal.

"Every four years, a new real-life supervillain event—that was the plan. Like the Olympics. Presidential elections. Allowing time to bask in the glory. Rehearse the next performance. Then Time Cap showed me a vision of 2016. An idiot elected president.

'Agent Orange.' He dominates the news cycle. Late-night TV. HOAP would get buried in the headlines. No villain could compete with this man's treachery. My follow-up would bomb. … As an alternative, I will introduce Objectifier at a pivotal point during the incumbent's 2020 campaign. The final nail in his coffin. HOAP, and his trusty sidekick, will rise in 2021. To steal the hearts and minds of an undistracted nation."

"Count me in," glows Tal, leaning on his acting skills hard. "And you're right—some sidekick I'd be, pushing around a walker. I guess if your offer still stands, I'll take that Time Cap. Heh. Heh. … Captain Curmudgeon wouldn't stand a chance against Objectifier."

While TB3 is cackling, Tal grabs James's Re-Lo with the smeared left eye from the worktable and pockets it. The room spins. What's the move? This Re-Lo might have power for a single blink and that's it. Tal has to make it count. He and James made a pact to let this Re-Lo die. Now Tal really regrets not dunking it in the vat of purple stuff; if they had, his options wouldn't be so limited.

"You're right!" barks TB3, oddly sharpening his vision. "Captain Curmudgeon doesn't stand a chance against Objectifier. Not many do." Skin forked with red lightning, TB3 unleashes an unexpected beam from his widened eyes. The liquid-like stream of nearly invisible light curves toward Tal and then envelopes him in a gelatinous bubble. How a sponge soaks in water, Tal's body soaks in the light. Every inch of him swells. And then he explodes in a cluster of flickering particles that flutter to the floor.

TB3 bends to grab the foam handle of a heavy-duty work light. "You wanted the spotlight," he scoffs, plunking the adjustable stand in the only available spot on the nearest table. "You got it."

Blinking on and off, it would seem as though the 500-watt bulb under the safety grill is trying to … communicate? It wasn't immediately obvious, but it should have been. Objectifier can turn people into objects. And TB3 just turned his own son into a work light.

18
HALT AND CATCH FIRE

The wall calendar in the control room is turned to October 2012. Which means Reva endured the latest full-body static shock to advance three months from the previous scene. According to the slash marks on the calendar, she's a couple of weeks off from the next circled full moon.

"Keeping people safe from them is harder work than expected," says TB3, gazing upward.

Overhead, the 360° video ring reminds Reva of the sports restaurant where Ant and his dad go on Sundays to revel in football. Here, at HOAP's headquarters, there are eight giant screens dedicated to each of the four villains. On his preparatory expeditions, TB3 must have hid a million cameras in every nook and cranny of the four cities, as a means to monitor the Fiendish Four's activities.

"Going on three months. ... Zero casualties to report." TB3 is monitoring Bombastic, who is inflated over the Pritzker Music Pavilion, twenty times the size of Millennium Park. It takes a camera from the other side of Chicago to fit his whole body in view.

Whoa. Talking to himself. A sign perhaps that TB3 has truly gone mad. Then Reva spots the portable work light on the big round table. "I'll set you at an angle so you can watch Daddy work. ..." He's talking to Tal, who apparently can use the 500-watt bulb as an eye.

Meanwhile, there is panic in the sunless Chicago streets. "People are scared. ... For nine more months they will live in fear. Longing for what they had, but took for granted. Not until all hope seems lost, will I be that HOAP—spelled with an *A*. I will give humankind back an appreciation for life."

Reva's attention goes where TB3 is pointing. HOAP's star-spangled suit is majestically hung in a cylindrical glass display before the Pocket Protector array.

"I could use some assistance," says TB3, speaking directly into Tal's shine. "I've been able to manage bee stings. Prevent the hoodwinked from walking in front of buses. ... But it's only a matter of time before someone gets hurt. Or worse."

A check of the overhead screens shows *Arrr*son rocketing toward the Loews Hollywood Hotel in Los Angeles, California—flames bursting from the jetpacks affixed to his pirate gauntlets and boots.

"Opportunity is knocking, son. Protecting four cities is too much for one man. You can keep lighting my workbench, or you can help me save everyone in that hotel. I can call on Tal5, but you're my first choice."

TB3 lowers into the full power of Tal's radiance. "Blink three times to join me. To be human again."

The yellow, powder-coated work light flashes its 500-watt bulb twice. Then, after a pause—a reluctant pause (if you can believe that a light can express an unwillingness)—the bulb blinks again to make three.

"That's my boy," snickers TB3.

Retina and fingerprint to the biometric scanners, and the shields on the red-lit Pocket Protector units slide open. New variations of *Arrr*son, Hoodwinker, Bombastic, and Misbeehive occupy the units between the five Protectors and Mimic Man (the previous models are on the pockets of the Fiendish Four). TB3 takes Re-Lo and Julioception from their holders. Re-Lo is then clipped on his jeans. Julioception is offered to Tal.

"Make the staff and guests sense the danger before *Arrr*son torches a single curtain. Bring the smell of smoke to the fire department's noses before the flames reach the carpet. Hollywood needs you, son. Your first leading role."

Fingers twitching, TB3 draws Tal's body out of the work light as though he were calling a genie from a magic lamp. Tal wobbles, making a great effort to find his bearings. The phrase "legs like Jell-O" has never been so appropriate. He blinks uncontrollably, sensitive to the fluorescents above. There is going to be an adjustment period after having a bulb-eye for the last three months.

For clothing, Tal is wearing the same sweatpants and TB3 Toys tee he had on going into the work light. His face is unchanged and still appears to have lived consecutive lives in these headquarters. He doesn't have an appetite; work lights don't require nourishment after all.

The Julioception Pocket Protector is Tal's for the taking, mere inches away in TB3's palm. "Any funny business and I'll put you in the home with your mother. A nice table lamp, perhaps. With a view of her final, unfulfilled days through a linen shade."

Tal pinches aimlessly at the air for Julioception, vision problems persisting. Power to control sight and the other four senses is at Tal's fingertips when it hits him—right before he got objectified, James's Re-Lo went in his pocket. And it's still there. "Let's hope you've got a little juice left."

"Huh?" questions TB3, clenching Julioception in his fist.

"Time to relocate!" Tal cries.

A blink and Tal is behind TB3, at the curved wall of Pocket Protectors. Tal nips Si Q from its holder and then vanishes. *He went to free my dad*, thinks Reva; and by doing so, she blinks to the cellblock.

The Fiendish Four's custom cells are geared up and ready for action. James and Tal5 are behind the very glass that imprisons them in the present. Tal5's cell is notably missing the charging pole; no wonder Tal5 lies dead on his back. Construction of additional cells, like the lockup made with crystal, hasn't started. TB3 has two presidential terms—and many full moons—during which he can prepare for a sequel starring Objectifier.

Tal's location-shift brought him outside James's cell. Si Q is clipped on Tal's sweatpants, and his veins flash with little blue lightning bolts. James scrambles to his bare feet, exhibiting more surprise in a pair of PJs than commercial actors who get cars for Christmas. Focusing on the security panel makes Tal's forehead visibly pulsate. With little strain on his brainpower, the cell door pops open.

Before James can start with questions, Tal relocates the Re-Lo from his pocket to James's hands. "There's a little girl and boy who miss their daddy."

"What about you? We go together."

"He'll just come after us with a full clip of figures," says Tal, securing Si Q on his fleece pocket. "Fighting him is the only way. I have to at least try."

Like a boxer entering the ring via teleportation, TB3

appears in the corridor by the cell with computerized bee smokers.

"Go! Now!" cries Tal, fixing his attention on the smoker units at once. Forehead pulsating, he taps Si Q's ability to interface with the system and max out every setting. The instantaneous, suffocating smoke drops TB3 to his knees. Tal then turns his Si Q-powered brain on Tal5, exciting the robot with a charged battery and an open cell door.

"Why haven't you left?" Tal shouts at James, who remains alongside him. "I've got this!" Every brain wave Tal can muster is uploading a directive to Tal5.

TB3 chokes on the asphyxiating smoke that clouds half the cellblock.

"He doesn't have a figure docked," warns James. "Tal5's powerless."

"I just gave him a Halt and Catch Fire instruction," replies Tal.

"That's not in his code."

"It is now." Tal says it with a nod to Si Q.

Steam explodes from Tal5's ears. He's already overheating. Soon James's creation will be a walking bomb in this combustible cocktail of smoldering fuels.

The dense smoke screens TB3's movements. Doesn't stop Tal5 from initiating his suicide mission—starting into the rolling gray mass.

"On second thought, maybe I will go with you," Tal says to James.

Whatever happens next, the outcome is a foregone conclusion: James and Tal5 wind up back in their cells. Is this simply more stimuli to lessen Reva's fear responses? More mental preparation for her predestined future as a real-life Re-Lo? Or is there some detail at hand that she needs to detect—in a smoke screen?

From thin air appear tens of twinkling stars traced by a dazzling line that connects them all like a celestial dot-to-dot.

No guesswork for Reva involved here. And James and Tal have enough comic book knowledge crammed inside their brains to place the spectacle. This is the visual effect when Ursa Double-Major conjures a mythological entity from a star constellation.

19
THE WATER BEARER

James and Tal stand in the cellblock corridor stiff as boards. An old man emerges from the smoke billows in nothing but a red wrap covering his private area. He's how Santa would look in the mirror if Santa were to eliminate treats and get on a strict training regimen. He carries a round golden jar that spills out an endless stream of water over everything and everyone. It cools the overheating bee smokers. Extinguishes the flames in Tal5's vents. And sends everyone afloat.

"Aquarius!" James shouts across the gushing waves to Tal.

Aquarius the water bearer comes from a constellation in the Southern Sky. Clearly to ruin that feeling of Christmas forever, as he goes from a swimsuit-model Santa who could slide down a chimney without magic, to a blowup yard Santa (a topless one that neighbors would complain about).

"TB3 is using multiple Pocket Protectors!" cries Tal, spitting out a mouthful of the rising water. "Stacking powers!"

Paddling in a circle, Aquarius positions his backside toward James, Tal, and Tal5; the stretched loincloth leaves very little of the water bearer to the imagination. The swelling continues until he plugs the watercourse between the cells and the wall.

Reva phases through the glass on her left into the arctic-cold cell prepped for *Arrr*son, getting clear of the Bombastic-size butt.

And then it happens. The loudest, longest, warmest fart ever imaginable. Flipping up the red loincloth, the tremendous force blows James, Tal, and Tal5 one hundred feet to the end of the cellblock. Dries the watercourse with its mystical dehumidifying power. By the squeaky conclusion of the epic wind breakage, only a few sparse puddles remain.

Reva phases through James's cell and Tal5's cell and into the open space that will accommodate more cells come 2020. James and Tal stagger to their feet while Tal5 sputters and sparks in a crippled heap on the floor.

TB3 approaches in typical human form and apparel, brandishing a ceramic table lamp. "Your mother would like this one, don't you agree?" he spits, hawk nose flaring.

The intent, fixed look that had widened TB3's eyes just before turning Tal into a work light is present again. Sure enough, left pocket of his jeans: Objectifier. Clipped next to Bombastic. Re-Lo and Ursa are on his other hip. A Pocket Protector combo that explains how he became an inflatable water bearer with impeccable command of his flatulence.

As liquid-light bursts from TB3's vision, "Tal the table lamp" feels like a strong possibility. James—either absorbing more heroism from the Re-Lo or acting on instincts alone—jumps in front of the amorphous beam. In the flailing save, James fumbles his Re-Lo. Instead of Tal, it's James's body that sponges up the surrounding brightness—James's body that explodes into shimmering particles.

TB3 takes another step toward the end of the corridor, vowing not to miss Tal with the next gaze. Then, wet spot. He slips. The table lamp goes flying. Smashes into a million pieces on the floor. In the awkward stumble, his hand swings upward, steering the light-specks that are James into the nearest object: the Re-Lo with the smeared left eye.

When Tal was a work light, the bulb was his mode of sight. TB3 would ask Tal questions and Tal could communicate back to him by flashing. Does that mean James can see with Re-Lo's pocket-shaped peepers? Hear through the side of his little plastic head? More importantly, can he use Re-Lo's powers? With a wink and a blink, Reva's questions are answered straightaway.

James just made a location-shift to four-year-old Reva's Pocket Protectors Palace Playset. When that exact Re-Lo was her favorite toy, she was convinced that it would smile and wink—even frown when playtime was over. Her mom thought she was crazy. But she wasn't. Not in the slightest. The Re-Lo with the smeared left eye *was* her dad. And she played with him every day until the day he vanished from the trapdoor chute.

PANDAS, Reva's autoimmune disorder, was at its worst during the summer before third grade. Everyone thought she had a serious mental illness—her family, her friends. Even Reva thought she was going crazy. She became a totally different person. Refused to get dressed. Refused to wash. Refused to brush her teeth. Refused to eat. Refused to sleep. When she wasn't screaming or saying something nasty to her mom, she would cry. Hours of crying. Outfits didn't change. Wouldn't leave her room. And it reeked, her room. The anxiety and obsessive actions went through the roof.

This behavior lasted for months and months. Until finally, she and her family got answers. A diagnosis.

Doctors didn't hand Reva a cure. An understanding is all they could give her. But having that ability to process the disorder was crucial in her fight. Reva's body gets confused when she gets sick. Makes her brain do funny things. She's not a crazy person. Understanding became her superpower. There are now measures she can take to manage a flare. People she can lean on for support. Strategies she can call upon.

That's how Reva would describe the sum of these time-shifts. Her dad's vanishing on the surface seemed like something that couldn't be explained. Couldn't be understood. But now she can process it. As crazy as the full picture may be. What happened to her dad wasn't her fault. And her instinct about his presence inside the Re-Lo Pocket Protector was right. This experience was designed so she would gain the power to act.

Reva's construct is interrupted by sounds of ceramic cracking under TB3's feet. "Heh," he snickers in Tal's direction. "Guess lamp wasn't your calling. I'm thinking you might make a good set of false teeth. Spend your days gnawing on the slop they serve your mother. ..."

Tal squirms against the end wall, on the floor with the defunct Tal5. Nothing is scarier than TB3 when his wheels are turning. The Si Q hanging from Tal's sweats is his only chance. It's either push Si Q's abilities to their limits or end up his elderly mom's bath sponge or, worse, her bedpan.

Forehead pulsating, Tal is able to wake Tal5 with an upsurge. Never had Tal expressed such delight when he had Tal5's face at age thirteen. Grinning prosthetic ear to prosthetic ear, Tal5 would terminate for a second dose of whatever utility just cleaned his system.

James built the robot primarily for exploiting Mimic Man's powers; Tal5 can convert to an incredibly wide range of human forms with fully adjustable prostheses. That in mind, Tal telepathically instructs Tal5 to stretch an arm for the Re-Lo on TB3's jeans. Then Tal watches Re-Lo get docked in Tal5's chest by Tal5's own artificial hand.

Tal follows with a series of commands: *Acquire TB3's Pocket Protector molds. Obtain geographic location of headquarters. Return with help—only if the probability of success is equal to or greater than 90%. And if possible, become self-aware.*

Before TB3 can react, Tal5 is gone, off on his mission with TB3's precious Re-Lo in his chamber.

"Pish!" scoffs TB3, searching the wreckage for a suitable object to be his son. "Your friend and Tal5 will be back in their cells for dinner. It's dino nuggets night."

"Your molds are gone," says Tal, brain feeling close to mush after taxing Si Q's power. "Tal5 has them."

"Where they are would require disabling an electromagnetic netting," says TB3. "Besides, one location-shift would consume enough power to drain the Energizer Bunny. Wherever Tal5 went, he's already dead."

"You'd be foolish to underestimate James."

"The human Pocket Protector? What's he gonna do, blink around the keys on a detective's laptop? Type out a cry for help?"

"He's a Re-Lo," says Tal. "You'll never pin him down. Give him enough time and he'll find a way."

TB3 whips out his belt like a wicked dad would to threaten a child. "What's that saying, keep your friends close, and your enemies closer?" Time Cap energy blast!

Si Q is blown off Tal's pocket. Objectifier liquid-light gaze! The brightness renders Tal as a cluster of light-specks that TB3 guides into his belt.

"James has until his power runs dry to enjoy his little girl," says TB3, pulling Tal through his belt loops, tightening Tal around his waist. "Then he and Tal5 will rot here."

20
HOAP FLOATS

"Crazy scene, huh?"

Reva spins around to find HOAP floating there. Sharing a presence with her in the aftermath of said "crazy scene." He's also here as a time-shifter, made obvious by his manifestation that echoes hers. It's the version of HOAP she encountered at Comic-Con, the version masquerading as a slobbish HOAP cosplayer.

"Imagine my surprise," says HOAP, "to discover a real-life time detective investigating me."

This never happened in the comics. Two Re-Los existing in the same time-shift. Evidently it's possible, as long as there are two Re-Los.

"It happened when I caught your father arming my would-be robot assassin. Aiding and abetting my ungrateful son. I time-shifted to see Tal's insubordination for myself, sparing them the effort of lying. That's when I saw you. The spectral sleuth. You were distracted by your father's arrival at headquarters. Justifiably so. ... If you had turned, you would have noticed me. How you perceive me now. As peers."

HOAP phases through Reva for no good reason, save for intimidation. Without anything approaching this in Re-Lo comic history, she is left to assume that a time-shifter can't hurt another time-shifter. That's not to say she isn't terrified.

"There was only one explanation for how you were in my past. And it's on your shorts. You look eleven, maybe twelve. ... Hard to judge the age of a see-through someone. That's seven or eight years since the day your dad blinked here. Meaning your trip would happen in 2019 or 2020. The only question was: How would you get a Re-Lo cast in the substance? Another of my early mistakes perhaps? There wasn't an explanation that made more sense. Your Re-Lo shirt at Comic-Con was what cinched it. I remembered you wearing it in these time-shifts."

HOAP glides down the hall into the smog outside the busted bee-smoker cell that buzzes with fried circuitry. "What a hassle this was to repair. ... On top of monitoring the Four. On top of recasting a Re-Lo to fetch Tal5 and your Pocket Protector dad."

Reva trails HOAP with a puzzled expression, processing what he told her. *He thinks I time-shifted from Comic-Con. Using the Re-Lo I bought at the TB3 Toys booth. That's why he took it from me. ...*

"Your dad was a victim of circumstance," continues HOAP. "I felt bad for him. I really did. ... The charging station in Tal5's cell is there so James would have someone to talk to. Heh. *Someone.* Tal used Si Q to make the robot self-aware."

The bee-smoker system coughs clumps of smoke in TB3's face. "... I was sneaking panels to the editor late one night. Hadn't built this place yet. ... But I was already working in the shadows. Night janitor caught me by surprise. Had no idea who I was. Threatened to call security. Guess my thieving attire was effective. ... I had a Re-Lo in my pocket. A cast from the substance that had failed. If it hadn't been a dud, I could've blinked the heck outta there. Still, I used it to my advantage. When I probed about kids, the janitor said he had a nephew. ... So I bribed him with the Re-Lo and went on my merry way. ... Turns out, that janitor was your father's uncle."

When present time resumes, Reva can say one thing for certain: TB3—in conjunction with his stupid purple stuff—took a lot from her family. Having to hover nearby and endure his phony sympathy makes her really, really angry.

"I can't figure out how another powered Re-Lo slipped through the cracks. No matter how many scenes I review. ... Every other failed cast was destroyed by my own hands."

Um, maybe you should've time-shifted to the origin of the Re-Lo I bought, thinks Reva. *You would've figured out that it was cast with regular ol' plastic.*

"Then it hit me. You were already here. In the past. ... Which means I don't prevent it. So why exert myself? Besides ... I fancied the idea of exposing my life's work to someone with writing chops. ... You could publish a best-selling biography. ...

"After I saved the world from the Four, relieved parents, not just in the four cities, but across the globe, finally showed their sons and daughters genuine appreciation. My deepest regret is that your experience was limited to a single parent. ... Hopefully now you understand why it had to be this way. ...."

HOAP phases through the custom cells designed for Hoodwinker, Bombastic, and *Arrr*son to the cell from which Reva is time-shifting in the present. The power to act wants to be deployed as a flurry of punches—straight to the kisser of this poor excuse for a hero. Fact remains: neither Reva Re-Lo nor HOAP Re-Lo would land a single blow in their spectral-sleuth modes. Reva has grown a little bit in each of these scenes. At the moment, her powers are stressing discipline. Reminding her that the fight is mental. She must resist the urge to tell HOAP off. And recognize when the right play is to simply let a villain monologue.

"Seeing that it's your birthday and all, I'll allow you to meet Orpha Mabe when we're finished here. I figure it's the least I could do before shifting you to this cell for the rest of your life. And what the heck, I'll even give you a Re-Lo. Just to prove that I'm not heartless."

A flash, and both Spectral HOAP and Spectral Reva are floating in the control room. Calendar turned to July 2020. Slash marks nearly caught up to present day. This slobbish HOAP haunting Reva is the version at the big round table. He's watching a YouTube review of a humanoid-lion action figure that plays on every screen overhead. The impassioned reviewer has a chubby square face, closely cropped hairstyle, goatee, and pair of browline glasses.

"Odis Posey," blabs Spectral HOAP to Reva. "Big-time Clash head. Hardcore toy collector. Cosplayer. Soon to be the real-life Objectifier. … I borrowed talents from a pair of researchers in Germany to solve his cell design. Advanced their technique called electromagnetically induced transparency. A process that turns crystal opaque. Objectifier's cell will trap his light. Prevent it from bouncing around. … You being at Comic-Con works out perfectly. Posey's got a booth there. I'll put you in your dad's cell, then blink back to unleash Objectifier on the exhibit hall."

Reva's proud of herself for staying calm. She just got the name, description, and location of HOAP's next target. *Okay, I'm ready to leave now*, she hints at her superpower. *Please don't make me spend another second with this guy.*

"Sorry for stringing you along through my life's greatest hits. For giving you the impression that this was all some elaborate superhero crash course. ... You deserved the therapy for the psychological torment I caused. So, for that, you're welcome."

And on that note—and not another note too soon—Reva exits the past for the present.

21
SpaceTime

"… Materials at nanoscale are stronger, lighter. They give scientists increased control of light spectrum. …" The "Nanotechnology in Sci-Fi: Fact or Fiction" presentation drones on and on. Sam hasn't lost even a nano-amount of interest. Everyone else's could be put on a missing poster.

Stella and Ant are engaged in a thumb war. The parents are practically drooling. Reva's mom, Amy, couldn't sleep if she were injected with sleep-inducing nanomachines. Mother's intuition is doing the job of six coffees. She's really worried about where Reva's been for the last thirty minutes.

"I'm going to check on her," Amy frets to a row of deaf ears. The lone reply is a snort from Ant's dad who tosses and turns in the cramped seat.

Amy leaves the theater in a hurry. Her departure from the group is not long past when their row becomes the site of a scientific anomaly. The air in the friends' view of the stage is tearing open. Ant is first to notice, letting his thumb get pinned easily by Stella's. Dancing wildly in her seat, Stella isn't wise to the rectangular black hole until her triumphant thumb disappears straight through it.

Before they can nudge Sam, an image appears in the

strange window. It's Reva. She's in a room with glass walls and there's a scruffy dude over her shoulder wearing a TB3 Toys tee on top of track pants. The friends recognize the man as James from the old pics Reva has of him on her phone. But it can't be Reva's dad. He's been missing for eight years. Impossible.

"Stella! Sam! Ant! It's me!" shouts Reva.

The friends stare at each other. Then at the parents who remain fast asleep. Unanimously, they reach the same conclusion: the nanotech presentation has sent them all to dreamland.

"You're not dreaming," assures Reva.

Sam whips out his phone and aims it at the rip in space-time. Leaning forward, he checks out the remarkable chat window from the reverse side. It doesn't have another side. He sees Ant and Stella talking to Reva as if the air between them were completely normal.

"Amazing!" Sam marvels.

"Put the phone away, Sam," sighs Reva. "This is serious. Something really bad is about to go down at Comic-Con. And we're the only ones who can stop it."

Reva eyes the sleeping parents, fixing on the empty seat where her mom had been sitting. "... Where is she?"

"She went looking for you," says Stella. "You've been gone for like thirty minutes. Where did you go?"

"... Long story," says Reva, who would swear that she's been gone forty-four years, not a measly half-hour. "I'm here with my dad. In HOAP's cellblock. Where the Fiendish Four are kept."

Not everyone has friends who are as trusting as Reva's. Another group might laugh themselves silly at such a preposterous story. Lie, exaggerate—the friends have never known Reva to do either. There's no chance this is a prank; this video-chat tech defies quantum mechanics. The main reasons Reva's friends aren't cracking up: Reva would never do something to make her mom worry. And she never jokes around when it comes to her dad.

"The HOAP cosplayer we saw isn't a cosplayer," says Reva. "He's the real HOAP. His secret identity is TB3. Neither one are who we thought they were."

"TB3?" questions Sam. "As in Clash Comics TB3?"

"Yes—"

"TB3 Toys TB3?"

"Yes—"

"Secret-underground-comic-book-writer TB3?"

"Yes, Sam. That TB3. He makes Pocket Protectors with this weird purple stuff. If you wear one, you become that character. The Fiendish Four were innocent people. TB3 turned them into supervillains. Just so he could be a hero."

"… You're using SpaceTime," Stella deduces. "Do you have a Re-Lo Pocket Protector made with purple stuff?"

"I do," replies Reva, eliciting expressions of amazement. "Listen, we don't have much time. The new Clash villain is going to be a real-life villain like before."

"That is serious," adds Stella.

"I'd blink to you," says Reva, "but the cells have electromagnetic shielding."

"Time Cap's old trick," mutters Ant.

"HOAP is targeting a toy collector named Odis Posey," explains Reva. "Short hair. Goatee. Chubby. Blocky head. Glasses that look like thicker eyebrows. I'd SpaceTime him, but you know how Re-Lo's power

126

works."

"You can only contact your besties," chimes Stella.

"Spoiler alert: the new Clash bad guy is called Objectifier. HOAP will have an Objectifier Pocket Protector for Posey. You can't let Posey touch it. Second he does, he'll be unstoppable. He'll turn everyone at Comic-Con into objects. Be wary of villain Pocket Protectors. Come in contact with one and the character will own you. Forever."

The friends assume that Reva's show of sympathy to her left is for a Fiendish Four villain in a neighboring cell.

"Get to Posey before HOAP does!"

Leaving the parents to finish their naps, Stella, Sam, and Ant spring from their seats and sprint out of the theater. At midmorning, the exhibit hall is comparable to a *Where's Waldo?* puzzle. In stark contrast to skinny Waldo's style, the friends are on the lookout for a slobbish masked man sporting jiggly spandex and a utility belt loaded with Pocket Protectors.

There are toys everywhere. Every. Single. Booth. After twenty minutes of navigating through elbows and extra-large guts, the friends find themselves lost in the crowd.

"Wait," Sam says with sweat circles on the armpits of his Nintendo tee. "Odis Posey. ... One of my followers goes by *Action* Posey. Hold on. ..." Sam pulls up YouTube on his phone. "Action Posey has a channel. It's all about action figures!"

"Okay. ... How does that help us?" says Stella, straining to view Sam's phone while getting knocked every which way by passersby. "He's got ten times more subscribers than you. Like he'd respond to a DM."

"Exactly," retorts Sam. "He's got that sponsorship money!"

Ant and Stella's attention follows Sam's to the sea of banners hanging from the rafters.

"There!" cries Ant, pointing past a column plastered with posters for a post-apocalyptic zombie movie. The logo from Action Posey's YouTube channel is on a long red banner—under the mark of the fast-food chain that paid for it.

Fighting waves and waves of people, the friends navigate toward the silhouetted action figure symbol as if it were the North Star. Pressing on tirelessly until the crowd spits them out into a pocket of open floor (which are few and far between). Another unsuccessful round of *Where's HOAP?* and the friends are beginning to wonder if finding a *Waldo* cosplayer is more achievable.

Refusing to give up hope, the friends suddenly get an eyeful of it. The round man with the hawk nose. On their right. Sticking out from the crowd like a sore—but very patriotic—thumb. It's so crazy that this cosplayer is actually the real thing. HOAP notices Reva's gawking friends and quickly ducks into the next wave.

Stella, Sam, and Ant must reach Action Posey ahead of HOAP. Ahead of that package under his arm. Gaining on him, the friends can make out enough of the box to confirm Reva's narrative. She was right— HOAP has a new Pocket Protector. The action figure's head is the *O* in *Pocket*, preserving the classic branding. Pictured on the cardboard backing is a black-suited character with a red *O* across his chest. It has to stand for Objectifier—the villain Reva warned them about.

HOAP squeezes out of the nerd-herd like he's pushing through a subway turnstile. He's beaten Reva's friends to the Action Posey booth under the red banner.

By the time Stella, Sam, and Ant catch up, the man Reva described as Odis Posey already has his hands on the new, exclusive Pocket Protector.

22
UNBOXING

"Open it!" demands HOAP, pushing the Pocket Protector package into Posey's chest.

Stella, Sam, and Ant commingle with the bustling crowd at the booth of rare and hard-to-find toys.

"Nah, man," says Posey. "You said this was a limited edition. Ain't worth a dime if I open it."

Most of Odis "Action" Posey's toys remain in the original packaging. The guy next to them is going bananas over an unopened 1978 Darth Vader with a double-telescoping lightsaber, making eavesdropping on HOAP and Posey a challenge.

"This one will be worth a lot more to you opened," suggests HOAP, exploiting the persuasiveness of a nearby car salesman via the Talent Master on his belt.

"What do you mean?" asks Posey, mindlessly pressing his thumb into the block of plastic that sticks out from the cardboard.

"These 'exclusive' editions let you become the character," says HOAP, lifting his slack belly to show off his collection.

The friends take note of Re-Lo, Si Q, Ursa Double-Major, Julioception, Talent Master, and the villain Time Cap. Characters that Stella, Sam, and Ant know inside and out. So when a band of moving pictures starts circling Action's head, the friends don't need a wiki page to tell them that Time Cap's powers are allowing Posey a view of a possible future. In the airborne vision, Odis is the illustration on the Pocket Protector packaging; a bushy-haired baddie with a neck battery, which supplies power to binocular-eyes through cables. He is flashing a scary gaze that shoots some sort of liquidy light beam.

Posey's rocket-firing Boba Fett and prototype G.I. Joe are two reasons among many why these toy fanatics miss the whole spectacle. The friends are at the Transformers: Gen 1 collection when the visual prophecy dissipates into thin air. Followers of Action Posey's channel aren't getting an unboxing video. Action is ripping this bad boy open.

"Don't open that!" screams Stella at the top of her lungs. It's not a sentence that hardcore toy people take lightly. When a hundred knowledgeable eyes land on the never-before-seen Pocket Protector, Stella gains the backing of the entire booth. "Pocket Protectors created the Fiendish Four!"

The mere mention of those superpowered terrorists gives Action reason to pause.

"Fine," snaps HOAP, yanking the package from Posey. "I'll demonstrate." HOAP rips the plastic off the cardboard. Then, gathering up his gluttonous gut, he locates an open spot on his belt to clip the Objectifier action figure.

HOAP turns his attention on the friends, and they meet Objectifier's gaze—a stream of liquefied light curving right for them. In a flash, the jellylike brightness captures Stella, Sam, and Ant, saturating their bodies with light until no more can be absorbed.

A silent shock falls over the show floor. The type of

quiet awe that typically follows a surprise demonstration or showstopping reveal. As word of three kids exploding into light-ashes spreads like wildfire, the silence is crowded out with screaming and crying. Setting off a stampede of panicked people toward the exits.

Action Posey stands there in great wonder. Never in his wildest dreams had he imagined such an action figure. "Give me that!" he says, plucking Objectifier from HOAP's belt. It brings HOAP much delight to see the toy get clipped on Action's pocket. "How does it work?"

Action flails his hands. What an Objectifier noob he is—unintentionally waving the shimmering cluster of friends toward HOAP. The friends' light-ashes are drawn into the nearest inanimate objects: the Pocket Protectors on HOAP's utility belt.

Meanwhile in HOAP's cellblock, somehow sensing her friends' predicament, Reva initiates another SpaceTime. The view to her friends' precise location is a live look at HOAP's utility belt and belly rolls. "What the—"

Three of the Pocket Protectors along HOAP's belt start swiveling back and forth, making the picture a lot clearer. "He objectified you into Pocket Protectors. ..." Reva deduces. The three figures slide up and down as if nodding.

Who is who? Reva wonders. Sam must be the yellowish-green Si Q; head shaped like an upturned butternut squash, glow-in-the-dark eyes, circuit-board unibrow, and blonde tuft of hair. Stella must be the brown Ursa Double-Major; purple hair bun, Big Dipper constellation face design. Ant must be the olive-colored Julioception; square head, slick side-parted hair, and

132

sharp white suit.

"Are you on HOAP's utility belt?" Reva's question elicits faster up-and-down movements from Si Q, Ursa, and Julioception. "Why would he turn you into his Pocket Protectors?" To answer this one, her friends shake side to side. "He didn't mean to? … It was an accident?" Ding, ding, ding! More up and down jiggles tell Reva that her guesswork is on the money.

Action's booth is suddenly dusted with stars that get traced by a dazzling line.

The celestial dot-to-dot effect is all over SpaceTime as Reva's view zooms out from the utility belt. "Stella, if that's you calling down a constellation right now, be careful. You guys have the powers of those characters, but as long as you're on HOAP, he does too."

Pacing the cell, Reva thinks outside the box. "… Sam, HOAP's headquarters is under W 51st St. New York City. As Si Q, you should be able to visualize the computer signals. I'm in the cellblock. Fifth cell."

Reva stares at the cell door. A nanosecond later, it comes unlocked. "It worked! Ant, I'm about to do some stuff that HOAP's gonna see coming three thousand miles away. Bring his senses as low as they can go."

The situation at Comic-Con is developing rapidly. SpaceTime shows a lot of bare chest and a XXXL skirt. From the celestial equator, Stella conjured a real live giant; namely, Orion the hunter. Raising his shield and sword into the rafters, Orion slices down every banner that hangs between him and HOAP.

Also using Ursa (which is also Stella), HOAP settles on fighting constellation with constellation. A beast from the hunter's weight class arrives in the same spectacular show of starlight. It's Taurus the bull, a real live version of the symbol from the Northern Hemisphere's winter sky. Taurus rears back and charges at Orion, stacking toy package after toy package on its long, razor-edged horns.

Action cries as his rare toys are all at once the "china" from that phrase about a bull in a china shop. This is his tenth Comic-Con. And very likely his last.

Following the scene on SpaceTime, Reva flinches when the bull's horns clash against the knelt hunter's shield. "Sam, I need access to the Pocket Protector units and a storeroom off the workshop." She has to assume that HOAP fortified everything after her dad tapped the vat for the creation of Tal5. "And while you're at it, disable every electromagnetic shield he's got. … Hang in there, guys. I'm on my way."

Reva turns to her dad, ending the SpaceTime chat. "First we destroy the rest of the purple stuff, then we get Tal5 back in the game."

James adds nothing more than a peculiar half-nod. Reva tries to put herself in James's shoes; how surreal it must be when your daughter, who you last saw wearing pigtails, assumes the role of your favorite comic book character. Her conclusion: she is the figurative ton of bricks that has just hit him.

Free from the cell, Reva darts down the corridor, pivoting left after Misbeehive toward the workshop where Tal5 was built. She brakes at first sight of the henchmen's red-white-and-blue suits. Luckily, HOAP's gang is facing the other direction, gathered by one of the long rectangular worktables. There's confusion in the ranks, indicated by the shaking helmets, shrugs, and open palms.

Doing her best ninja, without Re-Lo's ninja catsuit, Reva sneaks up on the henchmen from behind.

Through the assembly of carbon fiber, she's able to spy Tal5 laid out on the bench. His amputated arm is tied off with a blue-stained TB3 Toys tee, and there are no signs of life.

Reva measures up the suited simpletons who might as well be empty-headed robots. This is the perfect opening to unleash a Re-Lo super-strength attack. Instead of thinking location, she brings every location to her fingertips. As fast as a location-shift, the power of one lives within her fist. Giving a thrust, she propels a blast of energy that sends the henchmen soaring across the workshop. Their flight abruptly ends against the far wall, where they slide down into a scrap heap on the floor.

Now for the purple stuff. The storeroom in the corner is open sesame. "Nice work, Sam," smiles Reva. There couldn't be a person better suited for Si Q's powers than Sam. If there were any of Time Cap's electromagnetic netting, Reva is confident that it's been disabled.

Nothing stands between Reva and TB3's precious substance. Glancing over her shoulder at Tal5's body, she recalls the delight Tal5 expressed when the color blue was exploding from his arm. Tal5 had theorized that someone using the substance for good could develop the power to destroy it.

With zigzagging blue streaks spiraling down and around her arms to arrowheads on the backs of her hands, Reva can sense it—Tal5 was right. She can destroy the purple stuff. Laying her hands on the vat, she brings the substance to an instant boil. Like a magnitude-8 earthquake, the underground lair shakes underneath her and all around. For a moment, the purple tornado funnel reminds Reva of school, the science project she did in fifth grade with empty soda bottles. The funnel twists faster and faster until it's no longer visible. Then, as if it had never started, the quaking subsides and the purple substance vaporizes completely.

Wasting few breaths, Reva blinks to the Pocket Protector array in the control room. She snatches the oval Bombastic, looks him dead in his pocket-shaped eyes, and then crushes him to dust in her fist. Reva refuses to let the undeniable cuteness deter her mission, giving the action figures remaining here the same merciless treatment. RIP *Arrr*son, Hoodwinker, Misbeehive, and the backup copy of Objectifier.

23
MIMICKED

It's Taurus the bull vs. Orion the hunter. HOAP is powering Taurus with the Ursa Double-Major Pocket Protector on his belt. Stella is powering Orion *as* the Ursa Double-Major Pocket Protector on his belt.

With punctured toy packages stuck to its horns like meat on skewers, Taurus circles Orion, gearing up for another run at the Greek giant. Orion flexes his rippling bare chest, brandishing his mighty sword that made shredded wheat out of every banner in reach. To the enormous, snorting bull, the flamboyant hunter's red skirt is the equivalent of a matador's whipping cape. In a fury, Taurus makes his charge. The hunter swings his blade, slicing nothing but air. His shield lifts, but too late, as Taurus bashes Orion backward through hundreds of booths. Defeated, Orion transforms into a group of stars that die on-site.

"Pull them out of my Pocket Protectors!" HOAP barks at Posey, sucking in his gut to bare the utility belt. "Now! So I can destroy them!"

Action's skin is showing early signs of the red lightning. Which means the Objectifier on his pocket is taking hold. Soon the character will possess him. Fingers twitching, Action extracts Stella, Sam, and Ant from the 3in action figures around HOAP's plus-size waist.

While a bunch of "bull" happens at Comic-Con, Reva blinks from the control room to HOAP's workshop, where the incapacitated henchmen groan on the floor and James lingers over his courageous creation.

"I need Tal5," says Reva. "I'll come back for you." Before James can inquire about her plan, Reva is gone and the bench where Tal5's battery died is cleared.

As they're pulled out of the Pocket Protectors on HOAP's utility belt, the friends take a distorted form, similar to how they would be reflected in a funhouse mirror. Despite the temporary malformation, it's a relief to be human again. And to be rid of that overwhelming plastic taste.

HOAP veers Taurus around and paints a new target on the disoriented friends. Stella, Sam, and Ant try to make a run for it, but their legs are pins and needles, their feet are as heavy as lead.

Just as the peril seems insurmountable, Reva arrives on the scene in an explosive rush. Strangely enough, she's propping up a dead teenager who is missing the lower half of his left arm. The friends can't believe their eyes that are still adjusting from being paint spots.

Reva flashes a smile as the charging bull evaporates midstride and HOAP shrivels into the frail, eighty-year-old man that he truly is. There, in Reva's hand, sits HOAP's Re-Lo and Time Cap, freshly plucked from the belt that's currently lost amid the spandex gathered at the geezer's ankles. Radiating blue, the lines on her palm turn the pair of Pocket Protectors to dust.

One by one, Reva's friends sense the action figures on their pockets—and put two and two together. Reva blinked here, pickpocketed HOAP, and distributed his superpowered Pocket Protectors to them. Stella wears Ursa Double-Major. Sam wears Si Q. Ant wears Julioception.

"When we were on his belt ... how did you know who we were?" questions Stella.

"Call it a hunch," replies Reva, grinning ear to ear. "Si, I need you to fix my friend here."

Sam glances at the Si Q that he literally *was* a minute ago. Then his interest rounds on Reva and the lifeless boy hanging off her. "Don't you mean, Sam?"

"Exactly," states Reva. "Sam Izumi. S.I."

"Huh." Sam is sure that his initials can't simply be a coincidence, already cognizant of the bond growing between him and Si Q. "Si can manipulate computer systems. Not resurrect someone."

"This is Tal5," says Reva. "He's a robot that my dad made."

When Sam stops a minute and listens, Tal5's inner workings start talking to him. "Ohmigod."

The friends' jaws hit the floor as visible computer code prints a three-dimensional prosthesis that matches Tal5's other arm.

"Happy Birthday!" exclaims Tal5, coming to life. Tal5 is a magician's hat short of making Stella pass out.

Proud of his amazing feat, Sam struts about like a basketball player who just posterized a defender.

"Stella, Sam, Ant, meet Tal5," says Reva. "Tal5, meet Stella, Sam, and Ant." Like outmoded robots themselves, the friends stiffly give waves. "Tal5 has a Talent Master onboard." Reva pats the TB3 Toys logo on Tal5's graphic tee, under which a transparent figure with a shiny blue cloak and hood is docked.

Took him a minute, but Old Man HOAP finally has located his utility belt in the folds of floppy spandex.

He's not happy to find the belt picked clean of his special action figures. "Get them!" he hollers in a crusty old voice at Odis Posey, the toy collector who maintains possession of Objectifier's powers.

Posey loads up his dilated vision with a liquid-light gaze that he intends to point at the four friends and Tal5.

"Ant!" cries Reva. "Bring Posey to his senses!"

Emboldened by Reva's nudge—and the Julioception on his shorts—Ant strikes his signature meditation pose.

Seconds from executing his first objectification, Posey is suddenly aware that he can reverse the pressure from the Pocket Protector.

"It's working!" beams Reva. "Nice work, *Antonio*ception!"

Fighting the urge that would turn innocent kids into a double-telescoping lightsaber, PEZ dispenser, or Furby, Posey yanks the action figure from his pocket and spikes it against the torn packaging at his feet. Reva sticks Objectifier in Old Man HOAP's sniveling face as it dissolves in her glowing grasp.

Action runs away as fast as he can. The friends can't decipher his blathering, but it sure sounds like he's swearing off action figures for life.

"Give me Time Cap," breathes Old Man HOAP, "and I'll tell you where your father is."

"I know where my dad is. ..." Reva's confidence wavers. Is it possible that what she had read as shock was actually her dad being cold?

"Ah, you noticed," says HOAP, showing his decayed teeth. "I moved James ahead of your arrival. Your cellmate had a Mimic Man on his person. A spot-on stand-in for your dad." Reva had completely forgotten about Mimic Man. The rest of TB3's Pocket Protectors she either destroyed or gave to her friends. "And that stand-in is under a Hoodwinker spell. Brainwashed to execute a fail-safe plan. Designed for such a situation as this."

Amid the old man's maniacal laughter, Reva wonders what he could possibly have left up his saggy spandex sleeve. Then it hits her—the Fiendish Four! Without the luxury of time, Reva blinks to the cellblock. The situation is just as she feared—each of the four custom cells is unoccupied. She chain-shifts around headquarters, unsuccessful in her attempt to uncover a single burn mark, honeycomb, waft of hot air, or whiff of ancient leather.

Reva has only one method for understanding what went down here after she left for Comic-Con. So in her next breath, she's the spectral sleuth. Floating in HOAP's cellblock. Staring at four spiritless fiends in their suppressive glass rooms. Rounding the corner from the workshop is James—or the person mimicking James's exact likeness with a Mimic Man—moving like a man under a spell. An unbreakable Hoodwinker spell, according to TB3. James proceeds to unlock the four cells with a sequence of programmed presses on each keypad.

Freedom. *Arrr*son, Hoodwinker, Bombastic, and Misbeehive deemed it unattainable. They had long since thrown in the towel. As the Fiendish Four wrap their costumed heads around the open doors before them now, the person playing James drops his disguise.

Tal. Of course. Reva should have seen this coming. When he became TB3's belt, she assumed that Tal's fate was sealed. That his twilight years would be spent as his mom's bedpan. Jumping to that conclusion was a huge mistake. This was always about Tal; Reva had that figured out from the very beginning. The very first time-shift. TB3 was a creator, creating a monster. Mimic Man was practically begging for her attention from its unit in the Pocket Protector array. Why did she overlook its significance? Re-Lo wouldn't have. Because of this oversight, the Fiendish Four are once again free and Tal is in the wind, blindly acting under TB3's mind control.

Reva blinks back to the present—to the vacated cellblock in the vacated headquarters—and then to Comic-Con, where Old Man HOAP has spent the last minute eagerly awaiting her reaction. The rotten smile showing through the wholly American mask that droops loosely from his hairless, wrinkled, age-spotted head says it all. This is far from over.

24
THE PLANET'S PROUD PROTECTORS

Reva faces Stella, Sam, Ant, and Tal5, making a fist near the Re-Lo on her shorts. Blue light zigzagging down and around her arms, aligned with Re-Lo's color-changing arrow bands. "The planet needs our protecting."

"Reva! Reva!" cries Amy, leading a pack of parents in a full-on sprint across the evacuated exhibit hall.

It occurs to the friends, as they're overrun by hugs and affection, that there isn't a booth left standing or a banner left hanging.

"I'm so happy you're all okay," says Stella's mom, Lauren, with a waterfall of tears.

Over Reva's shoulder, Amy notices Tal5, who appears to be a lost thirteen-year-old boy. "Where are your parents, honey?"

"I don't have any," replies Tal5.

"Are you here with someone?" asks Amy. "A parent?"

"Only Reva," says Tal5.

"I'm sorry—I've never—" Amy rounds on Reva. "How do you know this boy?"

"Um …" mutters Reva, attempting to put Tal5 in total-silence mode with a look. "We met in the line to meet Orpha Mabe."

"Orpha Mabe?" says Amy. "She's your favorite."

"I know!" bursts Reva, eager to change the subject. "Dad's too!"

"We were woken by the screaming," says Sam's dad, Rei.

"We heard there was a giant guy with a sword. … And a … bullfight?" questions Ant's dad, Luke.

Occasions such as this call for a creative techie like Sam to step up. "Holograms!" he blurts. "… They were holograms—"

Piggybacking on Sam's genius cover-up, Stella launches into a rap.

> *A hologram of Taurus came*
> *right for us*
> *'Poor us!' we screamed in*
> *chorus*
> *Just like my neighbor Doris,*
> *it wasn't all that gorgeous*
> *At least it didn't … bore*
> *us—*

Someone has to put this freestyle rap out of its misery. "What Stella means to say," Reva interjects, "is that Clash's new villain reveal went horribly wrong."

The rest Reva leaves for her friends to explain away—how showgoers ran scared in every direction, convinced that the larger-than-life-size hologram of the bull and hunter were real.

Whether the parents buy the story that a flight of frightened freaks leveled all the booths and somehow tore down all the banners is not Reva's primary concern. There are more pressing matters to stress about. For starters, what should she do with Old Man

HOAP? And where is her poor dad now?

It's already crossed Reva's mind—blinking to James. But she hasn't shifted an inch. Re-Lo's powers can locate anyone. Anyone with a life force, that is. Which makes it hard not to presume the worse. She is troubled by the odds that Tal offed James when the use of James's likeness became disposable.

No one will believe that an eighty-year-old man is HOAP. No one will believe that the *Hero* of All People is actually a villain, or that there exists power-giving Pocket Protectors. No one will believe that the Orion vs. Taurus bullfight was real. Not even the toy nuts who had a front-row seat in Action's booth; their hindsight assumedly aligns with Sam's piece of fiction. Instagram will be buzzing about special effects that looked so real they were scary.

The smartest play might be shifting HOAP to a cell, giving Reva time for a regroup. Unfortunately, that bright idea is going bye-bye. Considering his new, old legs, Reva didn't think HOAP would get far. Yet by some miracle, HOAP is gone. From where she stands in this Comic-Con apocalypse, there is no sign of him or his skinsuit.

"Honey, what is it?" asks Amy, reading Reva's body language that speaks to something far worse than a total destruction of a pop culture festival.

Reva's internal dialogue drowns out her mom's worrying. *Can I time-shift to see where HOAP went without my mom or the other parents noticing? Do I have a choice?*

Before the next beat of her thumping heart, Reva is back in HOAP's cellblock. Resuming the scene when Tal frees the Fiendish Four and relinquishes his James disguise.

The degenerate degenerates take their first feeble

steps from their cells into the corridor. Between the antennae, stretchy suit, blindfold, and heat hook, there's a lot of rust to shake off.

"Take a few minutes to get your bearings. Rediscover your abilities. Talk about the …" Tal was about to say "weather," but they haven't seen the light of day in seven years … "spitball some doomsday scenarios." The suggested topic awakens a sudden passion in the group.

Functioning under the Hoodwinker spell, Tal makes tracks to his cubed-in bedroom adjoining the main operations hub. Reva doesn't stray. The keypad passcode is new, but as simple as ever: 4, 3, 2, 1.

Why isn't Reva surprised when Tal heads directly for the bookshelf filled with comic book back issues? Sitting on the middle shelf is her dad's old Re-Lo with the smeared left eye. An early cast from the purple stuff that TB3 had labeled a failure, but ended up providing powers from Reva's fourth birthday to the day it ran dry when she was five; the infamous day TB3 recaptured it from the trapdoor chute in her playset.

"There you are, James," sneers Tal, clipping the action figure on the pocket of his track pants next to Mimic Man. "Prisoner. Re-Lo. Prisoner. Re-Lo. You can't catch a break, can you?"

That's why I couldn't shift to my dad, Reva deduces. *Because he's not him. He's a Re-Lo. Again.*

"Time to relocate!" shouts Tal, with the telltale sign of villainous possession streaking his skin. Much to Tal's dismay, the catchphrase takes him nowhere. "Ugh. If your meddlesome daughter hadn't vaporized every last drop of the substance, I could give you a recharge. … Guess that means we're flying coach. You'll like where we're going. … Should feel right at home in

Dad's emergency bunker under Comic-Con. Maybe we can catch some tasty nuggets from the rumor mill."

Slapping Tal would be extremely satisfying. Even with an invisible hand. Reva gets as far as the windup when her sneakers are suddenly returned to the litter of stabbed toy packages and scattered comic pages. Squinting, she prays that the use of her superpower went unnoticed.

"Reva?" That tone. Her mom definitely noticed. "Reva, what's going on? You were scared—I saw you. And then … I didn't. For like a split second. … There's something you're not telling me. …"

Reva flicks her eyes at her mom, at the parents, and then at the Re-Lo on her pocket. She and her friends saved thousands from getting objectified into their phones, cosplayer props, or free swag. But it wasn't enough. HOAP escaped underground. He's resourceful and creative, if he's anything. Which makes him dangerous. Even at the age of eighty. With or without Pocket Protectors. His worst creations are free, and the very worst of which, Tal, is being manipulated by outside forces.

Then there's her dad—how can he possibly return to human form? She destroyed the entirety of the substance and the one Pocket Protector that could have reversed his state.

Sensing the pressure mounting on their new leader, Stella, Sam, Ant, and Tal5 take their places behind Reva. Pocket Protectors clipped on their pockets. Blue lightning streaking their veins.

"We have to talk," Reva says to Amy and the parents—on behalf of The Planet's Proud Protectors.

ABOUT THE AUTHOR

James Rad grew up a stone's throw from Plymouth Rock where he was always writing something—video game stories, comic strips, movies, and rap songs for school projects; see "South Carolina: The Colony Rap".

James still lives in Massachusetts with his wife and two children. His daughter and son are always writing something—video game stories, comic strips, movies, and rap songs for school projects; see "Not a Lot (of Glue)". James created the *Pocket Protectors* series especially for them.

Made in the USA
Monee, IL
27 February 2021

61077202R00090